Cheerleader By Chance

Reluctant Feminization and Transgender Romance

"This story is for you.

May it transform you into

the person you are and

transport you into a world

where your fantasies come to life."

BRIGHTLUCKY PRESS

Table of Contents

∞∞∞

Introduction

"Who said something about male flyers!? We're going to dress you up as a girl cheerleader."

This is an illustrated romance novella, it includes beautiful images inside. Enjoy!

My sister must've lost her mind when she introduced me to the squad. Yes, I was desperate for a scholarship but not to the point that I'd have to wear a skirt and parade with pom poms.

However, when I met the cheer captain... everything changed. Even my wardrobe!

Clutch your Pearl Necklace Tight and

Prepare for a Transgender Romance Ride!

Note: This story contains lesbian transgender love, feminization, transgender transformation, transgender romance, and first time with a transgender woman tropes. Some real places and people were referenced but the story is a work of fiction. The cover image is from Brightlucky Press.

I'm Lilly Lustwood and I'm a transgender woman. I'm a senior editor by day and I recall and write my romantic rendezvous by night.

Most of my titles deal with feminization. A fragment of what makes me find happiness in my gender identity, amidst the discrimination against women like me is my transformation.

When I look in the mirror and I gaze at my authentic self, I know that no matter what happens, I'm living my life and not somebody else's idea of how I should.

The clothes I wear, my long black hair, the fruity bath products that I use, the hormone medications I take before I go to bed, the sillage of my floral perfume, the surgeries I've undergone, and every step that I take with my size 12 Jimmy Choos, are all proudly from me...

...from my authentic feminine self.

Picture this...

- ❖ I have long and straight black hair and stand 5ft 6in.
- ❖ My alabaster curvaceous physique enjoys silk dresses
- ❖ I'm blessed with huge cat eyes and heart-shaped lips
- ❖ I want to share the rest but that's not very lady-like *wink*

Now that you know what your storyteller looks like, let's get to Cheerleader By Chance – Reluctant Feminization and Transgender Romance.

Free Vip Mailing List

∞ ∞ ∞

Before we get to the exciting part, I'm cordially inviting you to be a Lilly Lustwood VIP.

IT DOESN'T COST ANYTHING. All you have to do is Join my Mailing List.

I will be sending you FREE Exclusive Romantic Content that you won't find anywhere else.

My First Gift For You

Apart from that, I'll also send you Announcements of my New Releases and Promos.

I won't send you anything that's not related to my stories and I won't share your information with any person or entity.

CLICK TO READ FOR FREE

or Copy this Link -> stats.sender.net/ forms/er756a/view

Note: Please check your Spam or Promotions tab
if the confirmation doesn't arrive in your inbox.

Love Always, Lilly

Chapter 1

∞ ∞ ∞

I WAS IN THE MIDDLE of a losing battle against an invincible alien horde on my Xbox, my fingers stumbling awkwardly over the buttons, when Christina breezed into the room. The scent of her lavender shampoo wafted over me, a reminder of the girl she had once been, before college made her too grown-up for such things.

The sharp, bitter tang of a double espresso clung to her, proof to the all-nighters she had been pulling. College hadn't changed that part of her, at least.

"Still haven't mastered the art of shooting straight, huh?" she said, sliding onto the couch next to me with the grace of a cat. Her laugh was windchimes, light and musical, teasing me as always.

"Very funny," I grumbled, my eyes never leaving the screen. The aliens weren't taking a break for sibling banter.

"Not all of us can be geniuses like you, Chris."

She watched me for a moment, her almond-shaped eyes, the exact mirror of mine, sparkling with amusement.

"Well, if you put as much effort into studying as you do into this game, you might stand a chance."

The controller slipped from my grasp and I sighed, admitting defeat to the alien invaders. I slumped back into the soft fabric of the couch, letting it swallow me whole. It smelled of home, of countless hours spent here, a blend of popcorn, fabric softener and something uniquely Christina. I could almost taste the salt of my impending frustration.

"I've been trying. But, it's like my brain wasn't wired for this stuff."

She ran a hand through her brown hair, its silky length shimmering under the room's soft light. For a moment, I saw her, not as the golden child but as a sister, concerned and empathetic.

"You're trying too hard on the wrong direction. You're smart, just not in the same way as I am."

"Great, I'm 'different' smart," I said, my voice laced with bitterness. The silence that followed was thick, the tension winding its way through the room like a snake. The distant hum of the refrigerator was the only thing keeping us company. I could almost hear the cogs turning in Christina's head.

"You don't need to get an academic scholarship, you know," she said finally, her voice soft.

"There are other ways to pay for college."

"I don't want to end up neck-deep in student loans." The words felt heavy in my mouth, a bitter pill I had no choice but to swallow.

"Well, have you thought about athletics?" She offered, a hopeful glint in her eyes.

I snorted, imagining myself, short and skinny as I was, attempting any kind of sports.

"You've seen me, right? I'm about as athletic as

a sloth."

She elbowed me lightly, her warmth bleeding through our shirts.

"You've never really tried, Brent. Who knows, you might surprise yourself."

I shook my head, not quite ready to believe her. But I wanted to. Desperately. Her faith was contagious, a sweet melody that I yearned to dance to.

"I guess it won't hurt to try."

She grinned, her face lighting up in a way that made my heart clench.

"That's the spirit, little brother."

I groaned, rolling my eyes.

"I'm only younger by ten minutes."

"Yes, but I'll always be the wiser one," she shot back, her eyes twinkling. She rose, leaving a void beside me that I suddenly missed.

"Just think about it."

The day after my conversation with Chris, I found myself standing at the entrance of Spiritville Club, the country club where my mother

Sally, worked.

It was a sprawling estate, manicured lawns gleaming emerald green under the summer sun, the air heavy with the smell of freshly cut grass and privilege. I felt like an interloper, a stray cat that had wandered onto the wrong side of town.

I spotted my mother in her element, a picture of poised elegance in her business suit, the color of ripe peaches. She was negotiating something on her phone, the club manager persona in full swing. Her auburn hair was swept up in a neat bun, her sharp eyes flashing with determination. She caught sight of me and signaled me over.

"Brent, what are you doing here?" she asked, her surprise barely concealed.

"I was hoping I could use the facilities," I said, feeling awkward.

"I need to... I'm trying to get an athletic scholarship."

A myriad of emotions played on her face —surprise, concern, and finally, a hint of understanding.

"Alright, but be discreet," she said, her voice barely above a whisper.

"And don't mingle too much with the kids here. We can't let them know I'm letting you use the facilities."

"Thanks, Mom," I said, relieved.

"I promise I won't cause any trouble."

Over the next few days, I tried my hand at different sports. I donned crisp white polo shirts and shorts, the fabric chafing against my skin, a constant reminder of my awkwardness. I was a stranger in this world, a fact highlighted by my inept attempts at sports.

I tried golf first, the sport of the elite. I fumbled with the clubs, the weight unfamiliar and uncomfortable in my hands. I could almost taste the frustration when I swung and missed, the bitter taste of defeat lingering on my tongue.

The smell of freshly mowed grass and the faint scent of expensive cologne from the other players did nothing to improve my mood.

Next came swimming. I was given a pair of blue trunks, their fabric slick and cool against my skin. The pool was an oasis of sparkling blue, the scent of chlorine sharp and clean.

I dove in, the water engulfing me, cool and refreshing against the heat of the day. But my clumsy strokes and lack of breath control made it clear that I was no Michael Phelps.

Then, I ventured into soccer. The rich, earthy smell of the field hit me as I stepped onto the pitch, my cleats sinking slightly into the soft ground. I was given a red jersey, the fabric light and airy, a stark contrast to the weight of my expectations.

My lack of coordination was glaringly evident as I stumbled more than I sprinted, the ball remaining stubbornly out of my control.

By the time I tried tennis, my spirit was deflated, my body aching in places I didn't know could ache. I was handed a racket, its grip firm and sturdy in my hand. The court was a stark rectangle of green and white, the net a formidable barrier.

I donned a white polo shirt and shorts, my sneakers squeaking against the concrete.

Soon after, I felt the impact of the ball against the racket, a satisfying thunk that sent a shiver down my spine. The ball sailed across the net, and for a moment, everything seemed to still. I watched as it landed in the opponent's court, a feeling of accomplishment surging through me.

The sharp smell of rubber and the faint metallic scent of the racket filled my nostrils and that's when I realized I was grinning, a wide, exhilarating smile that made my face ache. The exhilaration was a sweet taste on my tongue, a flavor I hadn't savored in a long time. I was hooked, my heart pounding in my chest with a rhythm that echoed the bounce of the tennis ball.

Over the next few days, I found myself returning to the tennis court again and again. The bright orange sun would beat down on me, its heat seeping into my white polo shirt, sticking it to my back with a sheen of sweat. I relished the burn of it, the way it made me feel alive, my senses heightened.

I lost myself in the thwack of the racket against the ball, the soft grunt that escaped my lips with every swing, the way the world blurred into a frenzy of green and white as I chased after the ball. The court became my sanctuary, the place where I could forget about scholarships and disappointments.

Tennis was a dance, a ballet of power and precision. I found an odd sense of peace in its rhythm, a harmony that seemed to resonate with my own heartbeat. I could feel the rhythm, the cadence, the pulse of the game. It was a symphony of sound and movement that echoed in my bones, a song I was beginning to learn.

I began to notice the subtle nuances of the game—the way the ball spun in the air, the way my opponent's feet shuffled before a serve, the way the crowd held its breath during a rally. These details, previously unnoticed, now seemed to shout at me, adding layers to the game I hadn't known existed.

With every passing day, my swings became more confident, my serves more accurate. I tasted victory, the sweet and heady flavor of success. It was a taste I wanted more of, a craving that had lodged itself deep within me.

I felt the sting of defeat too, when a well-placed shot from my opponent slipped past me, the ball bouncing mockingly out of my reach. But even defeat had a flavor, a bitter aftertaste that left me hungry for more.

As the week drew to a close, I found myself standing on the tennis court under the setting sun, the sky painted in shades of orange and purple. The scent of fresh earth and the faint musk of sweat clung to me, a testament to the hours I had spent on the court. The racket felt like an extension of my arm, its weight familiar and comforting.

"I think I've found my sport," I told my mother that evening, a sense of excitement bubbling within me. Her eyes widened in surprise, then softened into a smile.

"Tennis?" she asked, her voice barely above a whisper. I nodded, my heart pounding in my chest.

"I'm proud of you."

For the first time in a long time, I felt a spark of hope. I was still Brent Lowes, the skinny, short kid who wasn't popular with girls. But now, I was also Brent Lowes, the tennis player. The guy who had a shot at an athletic scholarship. The guy who could prove that being *different smart* wasn't a bad thing.

Chapter 2

∞∞∞

THE FOLLOWING DAY, the familiar brick-and-mortar edifice of Concord Briggs High School loomed before me. It was the same old building, but to my eyes, it felt different, tinged with the anticipation of my senior year. I could taste the autumn chill in the air, the faint scent of dew-soaked grass lingering as I made my way towards the entrance.

I was clad in my usual outfit—hoodie and jeans, a pair of worn-out sneakers on my feet. They were far from the trendy clothes most kids wore, but they were comfortable and familiar. It felt like armor, a shield against the judgmental eyes of my peers.

Stepping into the hallway was like stepping

into a different world. The chatter of students filled the air, a cacophony of voices and laughter that echoed off the lockers. The scent of textbooks, a mix of paper and ink, was a comforting familiarity amidst the chaos.

I navigated the maze of the hallways, my locker number etched into my memory. The cool metal of the lock felt reassuring under my fingers, a tactile reminder of the routine I had become accustomed to. I exchanged a few nods with passing acquaintances, the extent of my social interactions.

"Lowes, still rocking the nerd look, huh?" A voice called out as I navigated the hallways. I turned to see Steve, a fellow classmate with a penchant for the latest trends. He was decked out in designer clothes, a stark contrast to my simple attire.

"Always, Steve," I retorted, forcing a smile. His laughter echoed in the hallway as I continued my walk.

Max's, my only friend's absence was a void that seemed to echo around me. His animated chatter about the latest video game, his shared enthusiasm for retro games and useless software, all were sorely missed. Unfortunately, his family moved to Chicago.

We had been the oddballs, the ones who preferred the company of pixels and code over people. Now, I was the lone oddball. I felt like a boat adrift on the open sea, my only companion the looming uncertainty of senior year.

When lunchtime rolled around, I found myself wandering towards the school gym, a place I had rarely ventured before. The smell of sweat and rubber hit me, a potent mix that seemed to embody the spirit of athleticism. I could hear the grunts and shouts of the sports teams, the rhythmic bounce of balls, the sharp whistle of the coaches.

I made my way to the notice board, my heart pounding in my chest. The paper announcements of various sports club openings seemed to stare back at me, a silent challenge. My eyes scanned the list, searching for the familiar word – tennis.

To my dismay, there was a notice about the tennis club. But it was not the invitation to join that I had hoped for. Instead, it was a regretful announcement about the suspension of the club due to renovation work. My heart sank, the taste of disappointment bitter on my tongue.

"Hey, Brent!" Coach Simmons, the burly, no-nonsense gym teacher called out as I approached the notice board.

"Looking to join a sports club?"

"Yeah, Coach. I was hoping for tennis, but..." I pointed to the notice about the tennis court renovations.

He gave me a sympathetic look.

"Tough break, kid. Why don't you try something else? Football, maybe?"

Feeling hopeful, I made my way to the football team. Their burly forms were a stark contrast to my skinny frame. I approached the team captain, a hulking senior named Jake.

"Hey, I'm looking to join the team," I said, trying to sound confident.

He looked me up and down, a smirk playing on

his lips.

"You? Football?" He chuckled, shaking his head.

"Sorry, Lowes. I don't think you'd survive a day."

The basketball team wasn't any better. They barely looked at me when I approached.

"Guys, I..." I began, but the captain, a lanky guy named Marcus, cut me off.

"Lowes, you've got to be kidding. You're barely tall enough to reach the hoop."

The baseball team let me swing the bat once. I missed, my hands stinging from the impact. The team erupted in laughter, their voices echoing in the air.

"Better luck next time, Lowes!" The team captain, a guy named Ryan, called out, a smirk on his face.

Each rejection was a blow to my spirit. By the end of the day, I felt like a deflated balloon. The taste of defeat was bitter in my mouth, a constant reminder of my failures.

As I made my way home, I couldn't help but

feel like I was back to square one. The hope that tennis had instilled in me felt like a distant memory now. I was still Brent Lowes, the skinny, short kid who wasn't popular with girls. The fleeting taste of hope was replaced with the bitter reality of my situation.

The weekend rolled around, and I found myself falling back into old habits. I was ensconced in the familiar cacophony of video game sound effects, the cool hum of the console a comforting soundtrack to my day. A half-eaten pizza lay next to me, the grease from the cheese staining the box, the smell of pepperoni and melted cheese filling the room.

I was dressed in my comfortable weekend attire - an old T-shirt and worn-out pajama bottoms, my hair sticking out in all directions. My fingers danced over the game controller, the buttons clicking under my touch.

The door to my room creaked open, and in walked my sister, dressed in her usual stylish jeans and top, a stark contrast to my disheveled appearance. The look on her face was one of mild disgust as she wrinkled her nose at the smell of stale pizza.

"Brent," she began, her tone that of a mother addressing a misbehaving child, "this room stinks."

I grunted in response, my eyes still fixed on the screen.

"Any updates on the sports scholarship thingy?" she asked, her curiosity getting the better of her.

"No updates," I muttered, my mood souring at the reminder of my failures.

But Christina, ever the persistent one, didn't let up.

"Come on. You've been holed up in here all day. Talk to me."

"I don't want to talk," I said, my tone sharper than I intended.

"Brent..." she started again, but I was past the point of patience.

"Fine! You want an update? I didn't get into any sports team. Tennis club is closed for renovation. Football, basketball, baseball—all rejected me. I'm back to being the loser with no prospects for a scholarship. Happy now?" I exploded, my frustrations spilling over.

She stared at me, taken aback by my outburst. Then, to my surprise, she stepped forward and wrapped her arms around me in a hug.

"Don't be so dramatic," she chided, her voice soft.

"I know I'm only ten minutes older than you, but that doesn't mean I can't act like your big sister. I made a pact when we were kids that I'd take care of you, remember?"

I felt my anger deflating, replaced by a weird sense of warmth. My sister, who usually teased me and drove me crazy, was showing a rare moment of affection. It was strange, but also comforting.

"I'm sorry for pushing you," she said, her voice barely above a whisper.

"But I know you, Brent. You're not one to give up easily."

Her words were like a balm to my wounded ego. For the first time in a long time, I felt a spark of hope.

Two days later, I was sitting in class when my phone buzzed. I surreptitiously pulled it out, squinting at the screen under the cover of my desk. It was a text from my sister.

"Dinner with parents after school. I'll pick you up."

Later that day, we were at Mario's, our parents' favorite Italian restaurant. She was looking particularly stylish in her trendy ripped jeans and a chic white blouse, her brown hair pulled into a high ponytail.

"What is it that you had been dying to tell me in the car?" I asked, my eyes scanning the street for our parents' car.

Before she could answer, a waiter clad in a neat black-and-white uniform ushered us inside. The warm, inviting scent of garlic and tomato sauce filled the air, and the cozy buzz of chatter was comforting. We were led to our usual booth, the worn leather seats familiar under me.

"Come on, the suspense is killing me!" I said once we were settled.

"What's going on!?"

She beamed, her eyes sparkling with excitement.

"I have good news."

Intrigued, I leaned forward. "What is it?"

"Do you remember Sarah, my friend from the cheerleading squad?" she asked, sipping her soda.

"Yeah, the one who got you into cheerleading," I said, recalling the girl with the high ponytail and bright smile.

"Exactly. Well, she called me today. They're looking for a male member for the squad.... And I thought of you!"

I choked on my soda, the fizzy drink burning my throat as I coughed.

"Me? A cheerleader?" I gasped, wiping my mouth with a napkin.

"Yes, you," she said, her voice firm.

"Brent, cheerleading counts as an athletic activity. You could qualify for a scholarship."

"But... cheerleading? It's so... corny," I protested, the idea too absurd to even consider.

"Corny?" she scoffed.

"You know what's corny? Being stuck in debt for years because you were too proud to grab an opportunity. You know what's corny? Wasting your senior year moping about missed chances. That's what's corny."

Her words stung, but I knew she was right. I was in no position to be picky. And yet, the idea of me, Brent Lowes as a cheerleader was hard to swallow.

"But I can't dance. I don't even know the first thing about cheerleading," I argued, grasping at straws.

She rolled her eyes. "You're smart. You can learn. Besides, it's not just about dancing. It's about teamwork, coordination, and yes, athleticism."

I sat back, my mind whirling with thoughts. Me, a cheerleader? The idea was ridiculous, absurd. And yet, as she talked, a part of me wondered if maybe, just maybe, it could work.

"Think about it," she said, her tone softening.

"This could be your chance. Don't let your pride get in the way."

As our parents arrived, their laughter filling the restaurant, I found myself lost in thought. The image of me in a cheerleading uniform was laughable. But the idea of a scholarship, of a debt-free future, was tantalizing.

As the night wore on, as we dug into lasagna and shared family stories, the idea of cheerleading kept nagging at me. It was a crazy idea, sure. But then, hadn't my life been a series of crazy ideas lately?

Chapter 3

∞ ∞ ∞

THREE DAYS LATER, I found myself standing outside the cheerleading practice room, my fingers trembling as I texted my sister.

"Alright, I'm doing it. I'm going to talk to Sarah."

The door to the practice room was heavy, the metal cool to the touch. As I pushed it open, the sound of laughter and upbeat music filled my ears. A group of girls and a few guys, all clad in the Concord Briggs High School colors of green and gold, were gathered in the middle of the room.

Sarah spotted me first. She was a tall girl with a bright smile and a high ponytail, her cheerleading uniform fitting her like a second skin.

"Brent!" she called out, waving me over.

The room fell silent as I walked in, all eyes on me. I felt a knot forming in my stomach, my throat dry as I approached Sarah.

"Brent, I'm so glad you're here," she said, her smile genuine.

"Guys, this is Brent Lowes. He's Christina's brother and he's interested in joining the squad."

One by one, the members of the squad introduced themselves. There was Jessica, a petite girl with a friendly smile, and Mike, a tall guy with a laid-back demeanor. There was Lily, a bubbly brunette, and Tyler, a guy who looked more like a football player than a cheerleader. And there were several others, each of them welcoming me with a smile and a handshake.

Despite my initial apprehensions, I found myself feeling oddly at ease. There were no smirks, no scoffs, no judgment. Just a group of students who shared a passion for cheerleading.

As the practice began, I found myself drawn into their world. The rhythm of the music, the synchronized moves, the energy that filled the room—it was infectious. For the first time in a long time, I felt like I belonged.

Sure, I was no dancer. My moves were awkward, my timing off. But the team was patient, guiding me through the routines, encouraging me when I stumbled. I was Brent Lowes, the skinny, nerdy guy. But in that room, I was just another member of the squad.

As the practice wore on, I found myself lost in

the rhythm of the music, the exhilaration of the moves. I was sweating, my muscles aching, but I didn't care. I was part of something, something bigger than myself. And it felt good.

By the end of the practice, I was exhausted but exhilarated. The smell of sweat and the sound of laughter filled the air as the team gathered around me, clapping me on the back, congratulating me on a job well done.

"Brent, you did great," Sarah said, her smile wide.

"I think you'll fit right in."

As I left the practice room that day, I couldn't help but feel a sense of accomplishment. I had taken a chance, stepped out of my comfort zone. And it had paid off.

I burst through the front door, my heart pounding, the adrenaline from practice still coursing through my veins. My sister was in the living room, hunched over her laptop, but she looked up as I entered.

"Chris! It was amazing!" I blurted out, my words tumbling over each other in my excitement.

She closed her laptop and stood up, her eyes lighting up.

"Really? You enjoyed it?"

"More than enjoyed," I said, my breath coming out in a rush.

"It was... it was like I was part of something, you know? Like I belonged."

She hugged me tightly, her smile wide.

"I'm so happy for you. I knew you'd fit right in."

"But I haven't met the captain yet," I said, my excitement dimming slightly.

"Tara. She wasn't there today. Sarah said she'll be there tomorrow to assess me."

Her brow furrowed. "Tara... she's a bit... strict. But don't worry. I'll help you."

And help me she did. We spent the entire evening in the backyard, Christina teaching me the basics of cheerleading. Cartwheels, back handsprings, jumps—it was all new to me, but she was patient, guiding me through each move.

The next day after school, I stood nervously outside the practice room, my stomach knotting in anticipation. This was it. The day of my assessment.

As I walked in, I saw her. Tara, the cheer captain. She was a vision, a fiery redhead with piercing green eyes and a no-nonsense demeanor. She was clad in a form-fitting cheerleading uniform, her hair pulled back into a neat ponytail.

"Brent Lowes," she said, her voice crisp and clear.

"I've heard about you."

I swallowed nervously, my throat dry.

"Nice to meet you, Tara."

Without wasting any time, she got down to business. She asked me to perform a series of moves—cartwheels, back handsprings, toe touches. Despite Christina's coaching, I stumbled through each one, my coordination off, my timing shaky.

Tara watched me in silence, her eyes assessing, her lips pressed into a thin line. When I was done, she crossed her arms over her chest, her gaze piercing.

"Brent, your moves are clumsy, your timing is off, and you have zero flexibility," she said, her words cutting like a knife.

"But we're desperate. So you're in."

I stood there, my heart pounding in my chest, my mind reeling. I was in. I was part of the squad. But her words stung. I was in because they were desperate, not because I was good.

As I walked away from the practice room that day, Tara's words echoed in my ears. I was in. But I was in because they were desperate.

And that was not good enough. Not for me. Not if I wanted that scholarship, that debt-free future.

So I made a vow to myself. I was going to get better. I was going to prove Tara wrong. I was going to perfect the craft. And I was going to be Brent Lowes, the best cheerleader Concord Briggs High School had ever seen.

The next few days of cheerleading practice were a blur of high kicks, backflips, and Tara's razor-sharp criticisms. She ruled the squad with an iron fist, her fiery hair as fiery as her temper. Her uniform seemed to be an extension of her body, her movements precise and unfaltering.

"Jessica, your cartwheel is sloppy. Mike, your timing is off. Emily, stop stuffing your face and focus," she'd snap, pacing the length of the field like a drill sergeant.

The jocks would sit on the bleachers, their eyes scanning the field, their laughter ringing out every time one of us messed up.

"Look at the cheerful gays!" they'd shout, their words carrying across the field.

Tyler was quick to shoot back.

"At least we won championships, unlike you meatheads!"

Sarah and Lily, Tara's sidekicks, were just as ruthless. They'd point out the slightest misstep, their eyes constantly scanning the routine for any errors.

"If we want to win another trophy for the

school at the national cheerleading competition, we need to be perfect," Tara would say, her voice ringing out over the field.

"And right now, we're far from perfect."

I was in a state of shock. I had known cheerleading was serious business, but I hadn't realized just how serious. Every misstep, every wrong move, was met with a barrage of criticism. I felt like I was constantly walking on eggshells, my mind racing to keep up with the routine, my body struggling to keep up with the demanding moves.

Then, just when I thought I couldn't take any more, Colby, Tara's boyfriend, arrived. He was a handsome brunette with piercing blue eyes and a winning smile. He was the quarterback of the football team, the epitome of the high school jock. He sauntered onto the field, his letterman jacket hanging loosely over his shoulder, his eyes only for Tara.

"Hey, babe," he said, wrapping an arm around her.

"How's practice going?"

Tara's demeanor changed instantly. The strict cheer captain was replaced by a giggling schoolgirl, her eyes sparkling as she looked at him.

"It's going great, babe. We're just wrapping up."

She turned to the rest of us, her smile wide.

"Alright, guys, I have to go. Keep practicing. Love ya, xoxo!"

And with that, she sauntered off, arm in arm with Colby, leaving us in a state of confusion.

As I watched them walk away, I couldn't help but feel a pang of resentment. But then, I remembered Tara's words. We needed to be perfect. And if that meant enduring Tara's criticisms, the jocks' taunts, and the grueling routine, then so be it.

A week had passed since I had joined the cheerleading squad and the novelty was slowly starting to wear off. I was adapting to the routine, my body starting to move with an ease that surprised even me. I could feel the grass under my sneakers, the sun on my skin, the wind in my hair as I flipped and twirled, every move becoming more and more natural. Tara's criticisms had lessened, her sharp gaze no longer lingering on me.

One day, as we were going through our routine, Jessica let out a sigh of frustration.

"I'm sick of doing the same old routine," she said, throwing her hands up in the air.

Tara rounded on her, her eyes flashing.

"If you don't like it, you can leave," she snapped.

Sarah and Lily, ever the loyal sidekicks, nodded in agreement.

"She's right, Jessica. We need to perfect this routine if we want to win."

Jessica turned on her heel and stormed off, leaving the rest of us in stunned silence.

I found her sitting under a tree, her knees pulled up to her chest. I sat down beside her, unsure of what to say.

"Jessica, I..." I began, but she cut me off.

"You don't understand, Brent," she said, her voice choked with emotion.

"Tara and I... we used to be best friends. We had a pact... neither of us would date Colby. We both liked him, but we promised each other we wouldn't let a boy come between us."

She took a shaky breath, her eyes welling up with tears.

"But then Tara broke our pact. She started dating Colby. And then she became cheer captain, and everything changed. She's not the Tara I knew anymore."

I was at a loss for words. I had no idea about Jessica and Tara's past. I had no idea that Tara had hurt her so deeply.

All I could do was put an arm around her, offering her a silent comfort. I could feel her shoulders shaking under my touch, her sobs echoing in the quiet field.

I couldn't help but feel a pang of anger towards Tara. She had betrayed her friend for a boy, for power. She had let her ambition cloud her judgment.

But at the same time, I couldn't help but feel a sense of respect for her. She was determined, ambitious, and she wasn't afraid to go after what she wanted. Even if it meant hurting the people she cared about.

As I sat there, comforting Jessica, I realized that cheerleading was more than just flips and twirls. It was about friendships, loyalty, and betrayals—funny how their world was so vastly different from how mine was—when Max and I would just argue about not being able to return memory cards.

Chapter 4

∞ ∞ ∞

A MONTH IN, and we were facing our first major crisis. It was like a scene out of a war movie, with Tara playing the role of the fierce, unyielding general. The gym was filled with tension, like a string pulled too tight and ready to snap.

The tangy smell of sweat hung in the air, mixed with the rubbery scent of the gym mats. My uniform felt clammy against my skin, sticking to me in all the wrong places.

Jessica hadn't shown up for practice for an entire week. After a particularly nasty argument with Tara, she'd quit the team in a huff. But she wasn't just any member of the team, she was our only flyer. Without her, our routine was incomplete, our formation crippled. The other girls didn't want to step into Jessica's shoes, scared of the heights and the responsibility.

Tara was livid. She paced back and forth in

the gym, her face flushed with anger. Her red hair, usually so perfectly arranged, was coming loose from her high ponytail, stray tendrils framing her furious expression. Her green eyes flashed dangerously as she turned her wrath on us.

"Are you all just going to stand there?" she yelled.

"We need a flyer! We can't perform without one!"

Even Sarah and Lily, usually her staunchest supporters, bore the brunt of her wrath.

"And don't think I don't see you two standing there, doing nothing!" she shouted.

"If you can't help solve this problem, then maybe you should follow Jessica out the door!"

The gym was silent, save for Tara's shouting. We all exchanged glances, unsure of what to do. We were a team, but without Jessica, we were incomplete. Tara's ultimatum hung heavy in the air: find a new flyer in three days or risk our chance at the championship.

I swallowed hard, feeling a knot in my stomach. I'd never seen Tara so angry before. She was a bit of a bitch but still possessed control. But now, she was like a tempest, unleashing her fury on anyone and everyone.

"I can't believe I have to do everything myself!" she seethed.

"We have three days, three days to find a new flyer or our dreams of winning the championship are over!"

And with that, she stormed out of the gym, leaving us in stunned silence. The echo of the slamming door was the only sound in the now quiet gym.

We were left there, standing in the middle of the gym, each lost in our thoughts. The weight of our predicament hung heavy on our shoulders. Without Jessica, we were lost. Without a flyer, we were doomed.

I could still taste the bitterness of Tara's words, her anger so palpable it was like a bitter taste on my tongue. I felt a chill run down my spine, a shiver of fear at the thought of failing, of not making it to the championship.

And I was part of a team that was falling apart at the seams. I could see the fear in my teammates' eyes, the uncertainty, the worry. I could feel it in the air, a tangible thing, heavy and oppressive.

And I knew, right then and there, that something had to change. We had to find a way out of this mess. We had to find a new flyer. We had to make it to the championship. We had to show Tara that we were not just a bunch of helpless kids. We were a team. And we were going to prove it.

I looked at my teammates, their faces pale, their eyes wide with fear.

I decided to take the plunge. "I'll talk to Jessica," I said, my voice echoing in the hollow gym. The girls turned to look at me, their faces a mirror of surprise.

Tara, in particular, looked like I had just announced I was from Mars. Her green eyes lit up with a glimmer of hope, her stern expression softening for the first time since Jessica's departure.

"Really, Brent?" she asked, her voice barely above a whisper. I nodded, steeling myself for the task at hand.

I found Jessica in her usual spot, on the bleachers overlooking the football field. Her beach blonde hair was loose, the wind tossing it about her face. She wore her cheer uniform, the same one we all had, the green and gold colors of our school. But she wasn't cheering, instead, she sat alone, her knees drawn up to her chest, staring blankly at the field.

"Jessica," I began, my voice shaky. She turned to look at me, her blue eyes empty.

"We need you back."

She laughed, a hollow, empty sound.

"Why? So Tara can keep treating me like crap?"

I swallowed hard.

"No, because we're a team. And we can't do this without you."

She stared at me for a long moment before shaking her head. "I'm done, Brent. Done with Tara, done with cheerleading. I'm sorry."

I spent the next three days trying everything I could think of to convince Jessica to return. I pleaded, I begged, I even tried bribing her with her favorite chocolate chip cookies. But Jessica was adamant. She was done with cheerleading, and nothing I said could change her mind.

On the third day, I stood before my team, my heart heavy with failure. I could feel the weight of their expectation, their hope, and knew that I had let them down.

"Jessica's not coming back," I announced, my voice barely a whisper. The gym was silent, save for the echo of my words.

Tara's face was an impassive mask, but I could see the disappointment in her eyes.

"Well, that's it then," she said, her voice flat.

"We're done."

The taste of failure was bitter on my tongue, like stale coffee left too long in the cup. The smell of the gym seemed to close in on me, a mixture of sweat, rubber, and disappointment. I felt a lump in my throat, a tight knot of regret and self-blame. I had failed. I had let my team down.

I walked out of the gym, the sound of my footsteps echoing in the silence. I felt numb, empty. I had tried, and I had failed. I had let down my team, let down myself.

I could still feel the sting of failure, the sting of disappointment. The taste of it was bitter, a sour note on my tongue. The smell of the gym, of sweat and rubber and defeat, seemed to follow me, a lingering reminder of my failure.

I felt like I was walking through a fog, my senses dulled, my heart heavy. I could hear the distant sounds of the school, the laughter and chatter of students, the ring of the bell. But it all seemed distant, as if I was in a bubble of my own disappointment.

I could feel the weight of my failure, a heavy burden on my shoulders. I could feel the sting of

Tara's disappointment, the bitter taste of Jessica's refusal. I felt like I had let everyone down, like I had failed not just as a cheerleader, but as a friend.

Chapter 5

∞ ∞ ∞

S UDDENLY, AS IF A BOLT OF LIGHTNING had struck her, Tara turned around.

"I've got it!" she exclaimed, her green eyes sparkling with a newfound hope. She pointed a finger at me, her red manicured nail looking ominously sharp.

"Brent, you're going to be our new flyer." I stared at her, eyes bulging.

"Me?" I stammered, my voice a squeak. "But I'm not...I can't..."

Tara dismissed my protests with a wave of her hand.

"You can and you will. We don't have a choice."

"But there hasn't been a male flyer before," someone from the team pointed out, the doubt clear in their voice. She shrugged nonchalantly.

"Who said anything about a male flyer?" she replied, a mischievous glint in her eyes

"We're going to dress Brent up as a girl."

The gym erupted in laughter. I joined in, thinking she was joking. But as I looked at her, I realized she was dead serious.

"Wait, you're serious?" I asked, my laughter dying down.

She nodded, her eyes gleaming with excitement.

"But I can't...I mean, I'm not..."

"Brent, you're pretty enough to pass off as a girl," she interrupted, her voice surprisingly gentle.

"And you're about the same weight as Jessica. It's perfect."

I stared at her, my mind racing. This was insane. Crazy. Completely and utterly bonkers. But as I looked around at my team, at their hopeful faces, their pleading eyes, I knew I couldn't let them down. Not again.

"Okay," I agreed, my voice barely above a whisper. "I'll do it."

The gym erupted in cheers, the girls clapping and hollering in excitement. Even Tara was grinning, her usual stern expression replaced with one of relief and joy.

The weekend arrived and I freed my schedule as promised for Tara and the girls.

"Hey, Brent, hop in," Tara called out, leaning over the passenger seat of her pink convertible to open the door for me. The three girls were an explosion of color, their outfits a clash of denim shorts and white tank tops.

My sister appeared at the door, her eyebrows furrowing in confusion.

"Hey, guys. What's going on?"

"We're just hanging out," Tara replied nonchalantly, her fingers drumming on the steering wheel.

A whiff of fruity perfume and crisp car air freshener invaded my nostrils as I slid into the backseat, the cool leather seeping through my clothes. The engine roared to life, the music from the radio filling the car and bouncing off the windows.

Tara's house was a mansion that seemed to stretch out forever. I took a deep breath, the bitter taste of awe on my tongue, my palms sweaty as I followed the girls inside.

Her parents, cool and laid back—the total opposite of their daughter, welcomed me with easy smiles.

"Make yourself at home, Brent," her mother said, her sundress swaying as she moved back into the house.

We didn't stay inside for long. Tara led us to a poolside cabana, where the makeover marathon began.

The first step was waxing, and she didn't sugarcoat it.

"This is going to hurt a bit," she warned, peeling off the first strip with a swift tug.

"Ouch!" I exclaimed, my grip tightening on the armrest of the chair.

"A bit? That's an understatement."

Next came the eyebrow shaping. Sarah held up a tiny mirror so I could watch as she plucked and tweezed my eyebrows into thin arches.

"You okay there?" she asked, a teasing smile playing on her lips.

"Yeah, yeah," I grumbled, trying to mask my discomfort with humor.

The skincare routine was a welcome relief. Lily took charge, explaining each step as she applied various creams and serums to my face.

"This is a hydrating mask," she said, spreading a cool, gel-like substance over my skin.

"It'll make your skin super smooth."

Finally, it was time for the makeup. Tara's hands were a blur as she worked, her fingers deftly applying a range of products to my face.

"You're doing great, Brent," she praised, her voice soft and encouraging. For some reason, when she was in cheer captain mode, she was a total bitch but during the makeover, I felt nurtured —causing me to appreciate her maternal side. So much so that I almost forgot how she called me a frog more than a month ago.

I allowed myself a small smile, my heart pounding in my chest. It was crazy, yes, but also exciting.

Tara's eyes were fixated on my face, her fingers gently massaging foundation into my skin. The scent of the product was mildly sweet, its texture strangely comforting against my skin. She was silent, her tongue darting out as she concentrated, a stark contrast to her usual brash demeanor. There was really something endearing about this side of her, something that tugged at the corners of my heart.

"Close your eyes," she murmured, her breath tickling my cheek. The brush was soft against my eyelids, the faint click-click of the eyeshadow palette filling the area.

Sarah and Lily were a constant chatter in the background, their voices melodious and playful. They were browsing through racks of clothes, their laughter ringing out every now and then.

"Hey Brent, check this out!" Sarah called, holding up a flowery sundress against her body.

"No, this one!" Lily countered, a red dress with sequins sparkling in her hands.

I chuckled, my eyes fluttering open to meet Tara's. She was smiling, a hint of warmth in her usually cold eyes.

"We're almost done," she said, her fingers gently brushing mascara onto my lashes.

A strange sensation filled my chest, a mix of nervousness and excitement. I was about to see my transformed self, about to step into a world I'd never considered before.

"Okay, open your eyes," she instructed, her voice barely above a whisper.

I did as I was told, my heart pounding as I turned to face the mirror. I was taken aback by my own reflection. My eyes, enhanced by the mascara and eyeshadow, seemed brighter, my skin smoother. I was still me, but there was a softness to my features that wasn't there before.

"Wow, you look... amazing," Sarah breathed

out, her eyes wide.

"Definitely better than I expected," Lily chimed in, a grin spreading across her face.

Tara remained silent, her gaze meeting mine in the mirror. There was a sense of pride in her eyes, her lips curving into a genuine smile.

"I knew you'd make a beautiful girl," she said, her voice barely audible over the pounding of my heart.

I felt a rush of warmth spread through my chest. It was a strange feeling, a sense of belonging that I hadn't expected. I looked at my reflection again, at the person I'd become. And for the first time in a long time, I felt genuinely happy.

Soon after, Tara shoved a bundle of fabric into my hands, her blue eyes twinkling with mischief.

"Here, try this on," she said, her voice was rich, and I felt a shiver of something so novel to me.

I took the clothes from her, my fingers brushing against the soft, silky fabric. It was a cheerleading uniform, its brilliant blue reflecting in my wide eyes. The fabric was cool and slightly heavy in my hands, the skirt fanning out like an umbrella.

I retreated to the adjoining bathroom, my heart pounding in my chest like a caged bird. The bathroom was larger than my bedroom, with a bathtub that could fit a small family. The scent of Tara's expensive vanilla perfume wafted through the air, sticking to the back of my throat.

I unbuttoned my shirt, wincing slightly as the cold air brushed against my bare skin. I hesitated before unzipping my jeans and stepping out of them. I was left in my boxers, my reflection staring back at me from the massive mirror that dominated the wall. I could see the uncertainty in my own eyes, the fear that was gnawing at the edges of my courage.

With a shaky breath, I picked up the cheerleading uniform. The top was a snug fit, hugging my skinny frame in a way that was both foreign and exciting. I wriggled into the skirt, the short fabric barely covering my thighs. I adjusted the waistband, trying to ignore the uncomfortable sensation of the fabric against my skin. I stared at my reflection, my mind struggling to reconcile the image.

I opened the bathroom door and Tara, Sarah, and Lily were sprawled on the bed, their laughter ringing in my ears as they spotted me.

"You need to tuck," Tara snorted, her laughter

growing louder.

"Oh my god, sorry," I blurted out, feeling my cheeks flush with embarrassment. I ducked back into the bathroom, trying to figure out how to 'tuck'. It wasn't something I had ever thought I'd need to know, and I fumbled for a while before giving up.

When I emerged again, Tara's laughter had subsided. She handed me a pair of pompoms, their green and gold tassels matching the uniform.

"That's your homework, Brent," she said, a smirk playing on her lips.

"Figure out how to tuck."

I nodded, taking the pompoms from her. They were surprisingly heavy, their tassels rustling as I moved them. "Alright," I mumbled, feeling a strange sense of determination fill me.

And so, we began practicing. I struggled to keep up with the girls, my muscles protesting as I attempted to mimic their movements. But with every failure, every stumble, I felt myself growing more resilient, more determined. I was going to make this work.

As the afternoon turned into evening, I found myself lost in the whirl of cheers and routines. I forgot about my awkwardness, my embarrassment, and focused solely on the rhythm of the chants, the movements of my body.

Despite the oddity of the situation, despite my initial discomfort, I felt...happy. I was enjoying myself, feeling a sense of belonging I hadn't experienced before. The girls' laughter, the rustle of the pompoms, the scent of the girls' perfume, it was all intoxicating. And I was more than willing to let it consume me.

As the final strains of Tara's obsession with perfecting the routine died, her mother called us down for dinner. We tumbled downstairs, our laughter echoing in the grandeur of the mansion. I followed them, still feeling the odd sensation of the skirt brushing against my thighs, my bare legs cold against the air-conditioned interior.

"Girls, wash up before dinner," Tara's mother, a regal woman with a head of blonde curls, instructed. Her gaze landed on me and she did a double-take.

"Oh, Brent, you look...pretty."

She sounded genuinely surprised, her eyes wide.

Tara's father, a tall man with a salt-and-pepper beard, looked up from his newspaper. His eyes studied me for a moment before he chuckled,

"I must say, Brent, you do make a pretty girl."

We erupted into laughter, the sound bouncing off the marble floors and high ceilings. I blushed, my cheeks heating up under their amused gazes. Yet, I couldn't help but laugh along, their infectious mirth pulling a genuine smile on my face.

We sat down for dinner, the fancy table laden with all sorts of dishes. The aroma of baked chicken and roasted vegetables filled the room, making my stomach rumble in anticipation. I was used to microwave dinners and takeouts—this was a feast in comparison.

As we ate, Tara kept giving me pointers.

"You need to wax regularly, Brent," she said, taking a bite of her chicken.

"And let your hair grow out. We can dye it blonde."

I choked on my food, coughing as I tried to regain my composure.

"Wax? Dye my hair? Tara, that's..."

"I know it's a lot," she interrupted me, her gaze firm.

"But we need to win this championship and you need that scholarship."

I could see the resolve in her eyes, the determination that matched my own. I wanted to argue, to tell her she was asking too much, but the truth was, she wasn't. She was asking for a sacrifice, a change, but wasn't that what I was doing too? Changing, sacrificing my comfort for a chance at a better future?

I looked around the table, at Sarah and Lily who were both nodding in agreement, at Tara's parents who were watching me with a strange kind of respect.

I took a deep breath, tasting the rich flavors of the food on my tongue, feeling the soft fabric of my borrowed clothes against my skin.

"Alright," I said finally, meeting Tara's gaze.

"I'll do it."

Her face lit up, a genuine smile spreading across her features.

"Good," she said, her voice filled with a strange kind of warmth.

"Welcome to the Gold Lions, Brent, or shall I say, Britney?"

We erupted into more laughter but deep down, I was genuinely happy. It felt nice to belong to a group—something I hadn't experienced growing up. As the dinner ended and I found myself heading home, Tara's words echoed in my mind. I was part of the team now, part of something bigger than myself.

It was terrifying and exhilarating at the same time. But as I looked at my reflection in the mirror, the cheerleading uniform hugging my frame, the hint of makeup still on my face, I realized something.

I was ready for this. Ready to embrace this change, ready to fight for my dreams. And if that meant waxing and dying my hair and wearing a girly cheerleading uniform, then so be it. Because in the end, it was all worth it.

Chapter 6

∞∞∞

THE SCHOOL DAY WAS A BLUR, physics and calculus swirling together in an abstract dance of confusion. I sat in my usual spot in the back of the classroom, my gaze focused on the board but my mind elsewhere. The equations on the board were just scribbles, meaningless lines that held no significance. The only numbers that mattered were the hours ticking away until the cheerleading practice.

My fingers tapped against the hard plastic of the desk, a rhythmless beat that echoed my anxious thoughts. My heart was pounding in my chest, a staccato drumming that seemed to match the pace of my nervous thoughts. I could feel the eyes of my classmates on me, their curious gazes filled with unspoken questions.

I couldn't blame them. I was the same Brent who had scoffed at the cheerleaders, who had deemed them 'corny.' Now, I was one of them, about to step onto the field dressed in the same uniform I had once ridiculed. The irony wasn't lost on me.

I looked down at my clothes, a simple outfit of jeans and a button-down shirt. This was my armor, my shield against the world. Yet, in a few hours, I'd be trading it for a cheerleading uniform, for a skirt and pompoms. The thought made my stomach churn, a wave of apprehension washing over me.

Yet, amid the fear and uncertainty, there was an undercurrent of excitement. A thrill that sent a shiver down my spine. This was new, uncharted territory. It was terrifying and exhilarating at the same time.

The bell rang, snapping me out of my thoughts. I collected my books, my fingers brushing against the smooth pages. The scent of the paper, the ink, the familiar mustiness of the textbooks, it was comforting. A reminder of the routine, of the normalcy that I was about to leave behind.

I made my way to the shower room, my heart pounding in my chest. The echoes of laughter and chatter filled the air, the sounds of my classmates unwinding after a day of classes. I could hear the jocks in the corner, their boisterous laughter punctuating their stories of weekend exploits.

Opening my locker, my gaze falling on the cheerleading uniform neatly folded on the shelf. The sight of it sent a fresh wave of nerves coursing through me. The fabric was smooth under my fingers, the colors bright and cheerful. It was so different from the clothes I was used to, yet it was about to become my new normal.

In the bathroom, I changed into the uniform, unsure if I could really parade myself in public in it. The top was snug, hugging my frame in a way that felt foreign yet not entirely unpleasant.

The shorts felt too short, the top too tight, yet the reflection staring back at me didn't look entirely out of place. It was a strange sensation, like I was looking at a different version of myself. A version that could be a cheerleader.

A deep breath helped me gather my courage before stepping out of the shower room, the hallway bustling with students heading home. The moment I appeared in the corridor, the chatter decreased as heads turned. I could feel a heat creeping up my neck, burning my cheeks.

"Is that... Brent?" a voice echoed from somewhere behind me. The question hung in the air, a loaded pause following it.

"That's a good look for you, man," a familiar voice drawled. I turned my head to see a few of the guys from the football team leaning against the lockers, smirks painted across their faces.

"Yeah, Brent, you planning on joining the beauty pageant next?" another chimed in, his comment earning a round of laughter.

My first instinct was to bite back, to defend myself, but I held my tongue. This was my decision, my path to a scholarship. I wasn't going to let them belittle me. Instead, I offered them a cocky smile, "Just trying to broaden my horizons, guys."

Walking down that hallway was like running a gauntlet. The whispers followed me, some snide comments, some laughs. But I held my head high, ignoring the whispers and the laughter. I was doing this for me, for my future. Their opinions didn't matter.

As I got closer to the field, the chatter of the cheerleading squad became louder. I could hear the music playing, the beat quick and catchy. The nerves started to bundle in my stomach again, a different kind of fear. But I brushed it aside, focusing on the rhythm of the music, on the task at hand.

"Hey, Brent!" Lily's voice carried over the others. She was standing by Tara, her eyes wide as she took me in. "Hey Britney!"

"You look... different," Tyler added.

"Different good or different bad?" I asked, though I wasn't sure I wanted to know the answer.

"Different interesting," he said after a moment, a grin spreading on her face.

"It suits you."

The comment brought a small smile to my face, easing my nerves slightly. I was here, on the field, in the uniform. There was no turning back now.

The field, a vibrant expanse of green, shimmered under the afternoon sun, the cheerleading squad's chatter filling the air with anticipation. The cheerleaders, clad in their school colors of green and gold, were scattered about, stretching and mentally preparing themselves for the practice ahead.

Tara was at the center of it all, her red hair a beacon of authority. She held a cheerleading manual in her hand, her sharp eyes scanning the pages before she lifted her head to address the squad.

"All right, people," she added with a smirk.

"We've got a new routine to learn today. So, listen up!"

She clapped her hands together, her voice piercing through the idle chatter, bringing an immediate silence. The squad formed a half-circle around her, attention focused solely on her. I stood at the end of the line, my heart pounding in my chest.

She began, her voice a rhythmic chant as she recited the new cheers.

"When I say 'Concord,' you say 'Briggs.' Concord!"

"Briggs!" the squad echoed.

"Concord!" she continued.

"Briggs!" came the response, louder this time.

The chant had a catchy beat to it, easy to pick up and follow. I found myself mouthing the words, getting into the rhythm.

"Great!" she exclaimed, clapping her hands.

"Now, let's add some movements."

That's when things got a bit tricky. Each chant

was accompanied by a specific movement. A high V for Concord, a low V for Briggs. Claps, jumps, and a myriad of other gestures followed, each one more complicated than the last. I stumbled through the first few tries, my movements a step slower, my arms and legs not quite in sync. But I kept going, my determination pushing me through each mistake.

Tara, the ever-vigilant captain, didn't let a single error slide.

"Again!" she'd yell, her voice echoing across the field.

"From the top!"

So, we'd start from the beginning, repeating the routine over and over until our movements flowed smoothly, until we moved as a single unit. My muscles ached, my body screamed for a break, but the sight of my fellow cheerleaders, their determination matching my own, pushed me to keep going.

An hour into practice, Tara called for a halt. We all dropped to the grass, panting and sweaty, but a sense of accomplishment filled the air. We were getting there, slowly but surely.

"That was good, everyone. Really good," she said, pacing in front of us.

"But now, we're going to add the final touch."

I felt a shiver of anticipation run through me. The final touch. That meant...

"Britney, you're up," Tara called, her eyes meeting mine. The whole squad turned to look at me, their expressions a mix of curiosity and concern.

We didn't agree to her, calling me Britney, but with my feminine persona, I thought it was only right. I rose to my feet, wiping my sweaty palms against my skirt. This was it. My moment to prove that I belonged here, that I could be a flyer.

"Remember, keep your body straight and your arms strong," Tara instructed as Mark and Tyler moved to hold my waist, ready to lift me up.

I took a deep breath, steeling myself for what was about to come. As the count started, I could feel my heart pounding in my chest, the adrenaline coursing through my veins.

"One, two, three!" Tara counted off.

And then, I was flying.

The world tilted as I was hoisted into the air, my senses consumed by the rush of adrenaline and the thrill of the moment. The sun was a white-hot disc in the cobalt sky, filling my vision. A gasp echoed around the field, quickly replaced by cheers of encouragement.

"Lock your knees, Britney! Keep your body straight!" Tara shouted up at me, her voice carrying over the cheers.

I focused on her words, forcing my body into the correct position. My muscles screamed in protest, but I held on. I was flying. I was really doing it!

After what felt like an eternity, I was lowered back down, my feet finding solid ground once more. The cheerleaders erupted into applause, their cheers echoing in my ears as I took in their proud smiles and excited claps.

"Good job!" Sarah exclaimed, slapping me on the back, her usual stoic demeanor replaced with genuine excitement.

"Alright, alright, enough with the celebration," Tara cut in, her stern voice bringing the squad back to order.

"We have a lot more to work on. Let's get back to it!"

The rest of the practice was a blur, the squad going through the routine countless times, perfecting each move, each cheer. We stumbled and fell, got up and tried again, the sun dipping low on the horizon as we worked.

Finally, as the last traces of daylight disappeared, Tara called it a day. We were exhausted, our bodies covered in a sheen of sweat, our muscles aching from the effort, but a sense of accomplishment coursed through us all.

"Great job today, everyone," Tara said, clapping her hands together.

"And especially you, Britney. Keep it up, and we might just have a chance at the championships."

Her words sent a warm feeling through me. I was part of the team. I was contributing. It felt... right.

As I made my way to the shower room, the cheerleading uniform clinging to my body, the skirt swishing around my legs, I couldn't help but feel a sense of pride. I had done it. I had faced my fears, embraced the challenge, and I was flying.

However, my disposition shortly changed after removing the very last feminine fabric. As I was about to leave, I heard voices. I recognized one immediately. It was Colby. The other voice, softer but just as familiar, belonged to Jessica. I paused, my heart pounding in my chest.

"Colby, you promised," she was saying, her voice teetering on the edge of frustration. I peeked through a crack in the door, my curiosity piqued. They were in the corner of the shower room, their bodies pressed close together. Jessica was in a button-down shirt and hot pants, her blonde hair pulled back into a tight ponytail.

Colby, on the other hand, was shirtless, his muscles glistening with sweat.

"I know, Jess, I know..." he was saying. He sounded almost guilty.

"I just... I need more time."

"Time for what?" She pulled away from him, her arms crossed over her chest.

"To break up with Tara? Or to decide who you're taking to prom?"

"Jess..."

"Don't 'Jess' me, Colby. You promised me. You said we'd go to prom together. You said I'd be your queen."

He didn't say anything. He just looked at her, his blue eyes filled with something that looked a lot like regret. It was a side of Colby I'd never seen before, a side of him that made my stomach churn.

I felt a wave of anger surge through me. Jessica was the one who had quit the cheerleading squad, who had left us without a flyer just months before the championship.

And for what? For Colby? For a chance at being prom queen? I had trusted her, believed her when she told me about her fallout with Tara, and now this?

I wanted to storm out of the shower room, to confront them, to tell them what I thought of their secret rendezvous and how unfair they were to Tara. But I couldn't. I was Brent, the boy turned cheerleader, the laughing stock of Concord Briggs High. Who was I to interfere in their drama?

So I bit my tongue, swallowed my anger, and waited for them to leave with their nasty secrets. The sound of their whispers echoed in my ears as I heard them walk down the hall, each word a reminder of the deception I had fallen for.

That night, I lay awake in my bed, the image of Jessica and Colby burned into my brain. I felt betrayed, not just by Jessica, but by myself. I had let myself believe in her, in her story, in her innocence. But now, I was left with nothing but a bitter taste in my mouth and a resolve to do whatever it took to help my team win the championship, even if it meant becoming a girl.

Chapter 7

∞ ∞ ∞

T HE WEEKEND ARRIVED with a knock on my front door. It was early, the sun barely peeking over the horizon, painting the sky in hues of pink and orange. I groggily trudged down the stairs, still in my pajamas, my hair a mess and my teeth unbrushed. I opened the door to find Tara, standing there in all her early morning glory.

She was dressed in a simple white sundress, her red hair cascading down her shoulders, her green eyes sparkling with excitement. She looked radiant, like the morning sun had decided to personify itself in the form of a high school cheerleader. I blinked, feeling a sudden rush of embarrassment wash over me.

"Good morning, Britney," she greeted, her voice filled with an uncharacteristic warmth. I glanced down, noting the shopping bags she held in her hands. She had come prepared.

"Hey, Tara," I mumbled, rubbing the sleep out of my eyes.

"Give me a sec, will ya?"

"No problem," she chimed, stepping past me and into the house. I watched as she sauntered in, her hips swaying in that confident, Tara-like way.

My mom was in the kitchen preparing her smoothie. She looked up as Tara entered, her eyes widening in surprise.

"Oh, Tara, good morning! What brings you here so early?"

"Just some cheer stuff, Mrs. Lowes," she replied, placing her bags on the kitchen table.

"I thought I'd come over and help Brit... I mean, Brent with some... preparations."

My mom looked at me, her eyebrows raised in question. I shrugged, just as clueless as she was.

"Well, that's very kind of you, Tara," she said, returning her attention to the pancakes she was flipping.

Tara beckoned me towards her, a mischievous twinkle in her eyes.

"Come on. Let's go upstairs."

With a slight hesitation, I followed her up to my room. It was a mess, clothes strewn about, my bed unmade. But she didn't seem to mind. She started pulling out items from the shopping bags, laying them out on my bed.

"Here," she said, handing me a pair of cheer shoes. They were white, sleek, and feminine.

"These should fit you. And I got you some dresses too, for when we go out."

She held up a couple of dresses, each one more feminine and frilly than the last. I gulped, my mind racing. This was real. This was happening.

"And this," she continued, pulling out a blonde wig from one of the bags, "is your new hair. It's a human hair wig. Cost me a fortune, but I think it'll look great on you."

She was so excited, so genuinely enthusiastic about the whole thing. It was disarming, and strangely endearing. I found myself smiling, despite the whirlwind of emotions I was feeling.

"Thank you," I found myself saying, my voice barely above a whisper. I could feel the weight of the situation pressing down on me, the realization of what I was about to embark on sinking in.

She looked at me, her eyes softening.

"No need to thank me, Britney," she said, her voice gentle.

"We're in this together, remember?"

I nodded, feeling a strange sense of comfort wash over me. Tara, the girl I had thought of as a cold-hearted, competitive cheerleader, was proving to be anything but. And as I stood there, in my messy room, in my pajamas, with a blonde wig in my hands, I realized something. I was falling for her.

It was a strange, unexpected realization. But as I looked at her, as I listened to her talk about cheerleading and dresses and wigs, I knew it was true. I had feelings for her.

I wanted to tell her about Colby and Jessica, about what I had seen in the shower room. I wanted to warn her, to protect her from the heartbreak that was inevitably coming. But I couldn't. Not yet. I couldn't bear the thought of hurting her.

So instead, I decided to try on the dresses, the shoes, the wig. I let her guide me, teach me, nurture me.

"Okay, Britney," she began, her voice filled with a contagious excitement as she unzipped the first bag.

"Let's get you dolled up."

The first dress she pulled out was a soft pastel pink, a sleeveless number with a sweetheart neckline and a flared skirt. It was delicate and feminine, and I found myself hesitating, my heart pounding in my chest as I took it from her.

"You can do this," she encouraged, her green eyes sparkling.

"You look amazing."

With a deep breath, I slipped into the dress. The fabric felt soft against my skin, the skirt swishing around my legs as I moved. I looked at myself in the mirror, my eyes wide. The dress fit perfectly, hugging my body in all the right places. I could hardly recognize myself.

She clapped her hands, her face lighting up.

"You look so pretty, Britney!" she exclaimed, her words bringing a blush to my cheeks. I couldn't help but smile at her enthusiasm.

The second dress was a vibrant red, a bodycon style that clung to my figure. It was a little more daring, a little more bold. But as I zipped it up, I couldn't deny that it looked good.

"Wow," Tara breathed, her eyes wide as she

took in my appearance.

"You look... wow."

I blushed, feeling a strange sense of pride. I was doing this for the team, for the championship, for my scholarship. But at that moment, I was also doing it for Tara.

The third dress was a simple black one, elegant and sophisticated. It had long sleeves and a round neckline, the skirt falling just above my knees. It was classy, a perfect outfit for a night out.

"You look so elegant," she commented, her eyes shining with approval.

"Like a real lady."

I laughed, feeling a strange sense of joy. I was enjoying this, the dressing up, the transformation. It was fun, liberating even. And her words, her compliments, they made me feel... special.

The last dress was a beautiful midnight blue, a strapless number with a plunging neckline and a long, flowing skirt. It was stunning, a real show-stopper. And as I slipped it on, I felt like a princess.

"You look absolutely breathtaking," she whispered, her voice filled with awe. She reached out, tucking a loose strand of my blonde wig behind my ear.

"You're beautiful."

Her words hit me like a punch to the gut. I looked at her, my heart pounding in my chest. I was falling for her, hard and fast. And as I stood there, in a stunning blue dress, with her eyes on me, I knew I was in deep trouble.

Tara's final pick was a shocking pink crop top, the fabric hugging my chest tightly, paired with a pleated mini skirt that ended just above my knees. It was a bold choice, one that made my heart pound with a mix of anticipation and anxiety. As I changed into it, I felt a sense of liberation wash over me. I felt free, I felt confident, I felt... right.

"Wow," she breathed out as she took in my appearance. Her eyes held a different spark this time, one that made my stomach flutter.

"You're so pretty," she whispered, her hand reaching out to gently stroke my cheek.

Before I could respond, her lips were on mine, a soft, sweet kiss that made my heart race. It was unexpected, surprising, but not unwelcome. I kissed her back, my hands instinctively going to her waist.

"I'm sorry," she said, pulling back after a moment. Her cheeks were flushed, her eyes wide.

"I shouldn't have..."

I wanted to tell her it was okay, that I wanted her to kiss me, that I wanted more. But before I could, she was pulling me towards the door, saying, "Let's get some ice cream."

"But I'm in girl clothes, and a wig," I protested, my voice faltering as I realized what she was suggesting.

"And my mom will..."

"We'll sneak out," she interrupted, her eyes sparkling with mischief.

"Come on, it'll be fun."

I was nervous, terrified even. But there was something about her, something about the way she looked at me, the way she touched me, that made me want to throw caution to the wind. So I let her lead me, let her pull me towards a world I never thought I would enter.

We ran out of my house, our laughter filling the air as we sprinted towards Tara's pink convertible. The thrill of the chase, of being so bold, was exhilarating. As we jumped into the car, Tara let out a triumphant yell, her hand squeezing mine as she stepped on the gas.

We arrived at the mall, me still dressed in my girl clothes, my blonde wig perfectly styled. I felt a rush of fear as we stepped inside, but she was by my side, her hand holding mine, her smile encouraging me.

Walking through the mall, I felt eyes on me. But instead of the scorn or mockery I was expecting, I was met with compliments.

"You look amazing!" a teenage girl exclaimed, her eyes wide with admiration. A group of guys turned to watch us as we walked past, their eyes filled with appreciation. I even caught a woman looking at me with envy.

It was strange, being on the receiving end of such attention. But I was not uncomfortable, not even a bit. In fact, I was loving it. The compliments, the stares, they made me feel special, they made me feel beautiful.

Tara and I were like two hot girlfriends, out on a lunch date. We shopped, we ate, we laughed. It was a day full of fun, a day I would always remember. Because it was the day I truly felt like myself, the day I realized that I wasn't just playing a role.

I was Britney. And I was beautiful.

Three days later, during practice, I noticed Tara seemed off. The usually vibrant cheerleader was subdued, her movements lacking their usual flair. Concern gnawing at me, I approached her.

"You okay?" I asked, my voice soft, my heart pounding in my chest.

She looked at me, her eyes lacking their usual sparkle.

"My computer teacher told me I'm failing," she confessed, her voice barely above a whisper.

"I'm good with computers," I offered, my mind racing for ways to help.

"Tell me what's the issue."

"No, it's fine," she dismissed, her shoulders slumping. But I could see in her eyes it was anything but fine.

I couldn't bear to see her like this.

"No, it's not fine," I said firmly, my hands instinctively reaching for hers.

"Let's fix this."

She looked at me, her eyes wide and vulnerable.

"Really?" she asked, her voice hopeful.

"Really," I affirmed, giving her hand a gentle squeeze.

So, after practice, we headed to her house. I

was nervous, not just because I was entering the mansion of the head cheerleader, but also because I was about to see a side of Tara that no one else had seen. I was about to help her, to be there for her when she needed someone the most.

Her mom welcomed us at the door, her eyes warm as she invited me in.

"Brent, so nice to see you again," she greeted, her voice filled with genuine warmth.

"Nice to see you too, Mrs. Adams," I replied, giving her a polite smile.

Inside, Tara and I settled in her room, her computer assignment spread out before us. As I explained different concepts to her, her eyebrows furrowed in concentration. Her mom occasionally popped her head in, offering us snacks and drinks.

"Would you two like some cookies? I just baked them," she'd say, or, "I made some lemonade if you're thirsty."

She and I worked well into the evening. Every time she grasped a concept, her eyes would light up, and she'd give me this smile that made my heart pound. By midnight, we were both exhausted, but her project was complete.

She turned to me, her eyes shining with gratitude.

"Thank you. I couldn't have done this without you," she said, her voice sincere.

Before I could think, I pulled her into a hug. She fit perfectly against me, her body warm and comforting—her scent filling my nostrils. It felt right, holding her like this. But there was a tension in the air, a tension that made my heart pound and my breath hitch. Soon after, our faces were just inches apart, but then I pulled away.

"I should go," I whispered, pulling away. Tara nodded, her cheeks flushed.

As I walked home that night, my mind was filled with thoughts of Tara. Of her smile, her laughter, her gratitude. I thought of how amazing she was, how strong and brave and beautiful. And I thought of Colby, of how he could cheat on someone as wonderful as Tara. It made my blood boil, made my heart ache.

But most of all, I thought of how lucky I was. Lucky to have met her, lucky to have gotten to know her, lucky to have been able to help her. And I knew then, at that moment, that I was falling for her. Falling hard and fast and without any hope of stopping.

And I didn't want to stop. Because falling for Tara, being there for her, was the most beautiful thing I had ever experienced. And I wouldn't trade it for anything in the world.

Chapter 8

∞∞∞

A WEEK LATER, I was in full Britney mode. My wig was glued on securely, a trick I'd picked up from one of those YouTube beauty gurus. The cheerleading team had gotten used to my feminine persona every time we practiced, now referring to me as Britney. It was a strange kind of acceptance, one that both warmed my heart and sent a shiver of apprehension down my spine.

The sun was high in the sky, casting a warm glow on the cheerleading field. I was wearing a crop top, which clung to my frame, and a pleated cheer skirt. The fabric rustled against my legs as I moved, a constant reminder of the drastic change I'd undergone. A pair of white cheerleading shoes

CHEERLEADER BY CHANCE: RELUCTANT FEMINIZATION...

that Tara bought me hugged my feet, their bright laces a stark contrast against the grassy field.

As I stood there, feeling the wind playing with the strands of my wig, I caught sight of a group of jocks approaching the field. They were led by Colby, his athletic form radiating an aura of arrogance. The sight of him sparked a flicker of rage within me, but I swallowed it down, focusing on maintaining my new persona.

Their laughter echoed across the field, obnoxious and cruel.

"Well, well, if it isn't the sissy cheerleader," he sneered, his eyes glinting with amusement. His buddies laughed, their jests fueled by ignorance and prejudice.

A cold fury washed over me, but I held my tongue. There was a bigger picture here, a goal that was far more important than satisfying my desire to punch Colby in the face.

Tara, however, wasn't as patient. Her face was flushed with anger as she stepped forward, her eyes blazing. "Shut up!" she snapped.

"You're just jealous because Britney's going to bring honor to the school, unlike you losers who wouldn't even have the chance to reach the semifinals."

His laughter died down, replaced by a scowl. But Tara wasn't done.

"And besides," she continued, her voice dripping with venom, "At least she has the guts to be herself, unlike some people."

The field fell silent, the tension palpable. Colby stared at Tara, his expression unreadable. Then, he turned around and walked away, his buddies following him like lost puppies.

Despite the anger still simmering within me, I felt a rush of gratitude towards Tara.

"Thanks," I told her, my voice soft.

She shrugged, as if it was nothing.

"We're a team, Britney. We stick up for each other."

With that, we resumed practice, our movements sharper, our chants louder. "L-I-O-N-S, lions, let's confess! We're the best, no contest!" Our voices echoed across the field, a testament to our determination and unity.

After practice, I headed back to the shower room, my body aching from the intense workout. The scent of sweat and deodorant filled the air, a stark contrast to the fresh outdoor breeze I had grown accustomed to. I was still in my cheerleading outfit, the skirt swishing around my legs as I moved.

As I entered the shower room, I heard voices. I recognized them instantly—Colby and Jessica. My heart pounded in my chest as I listened to their conversation, my anger flaring up once again.

"I thought you said you were going to break up with her," Jessica whined, her voice echoing off the shower room walls.

"I will, I will," Colby assured her. "Trust me... come on babe, give me a blowjob."

I couldn't take it anymore. I stormed out of the cubicle, my hands clenched into fists. "You lying, cheating jerk!" I shouted, my voice echoing in the enclosed space.

He turned to me, surprise evident on his face. But it quickly morphed into a sneer.

"What do you care, *Fagney*?"

That sneer was the breaking point. The anger that had been simmering within me erupted, blazing hot and fierce. I lunged at him, my fist cutting through the air and connecting with his jaw with a satisfying thud. He grunted, reeling back, his hand instinctively flying to his face.

The shower room erupted into chaos. Shouts filled the air as football players entered, their wide eyes fixed on the spectacle unfolding before them. Jessica let out a horrified gasp, her hands flying to her mouth, her eyes round as saucers.

Colby staggered, shaking off the initial shock of my punch. His surprise turned into fury, his eyes blazing. With a guttural growl, he lunged at me, his fist swinging towards my face. But I was quicker. I sidestepped his punch, and with all the strength I could muster, I slammed my fist into his stomach. He doubled over with a groan, his hands clutching his belly.

That was it. I lunged at him, my fist connecting with his jaw. He grunted in surprise, stumbling backward. The locker room was suddenly filled with shouts and gasps as everyone gathered to watch the spectacle.

I was vaguely aware of Jessica's horrified shriek, and the cheer squad rushing in, their faces filled with shock. But all I could focus on was Colby, and the fury that was burning within me.

"You have the best girlfriend in the world, and you choose to cheat on her with Jessica?" I spat, my voice echoing off the shower room walls. I could see the surprise and guilt flashing in his eyes, but I didn't care. He deserved every bit of it.

Jessica tried to slink away, her face burning with embarrassment, but Sarah and Lily blocked her way, their expressions fierce. Tara, meanwhile, had turned as pale as a ghost. She looked at me, then at Colby, and then, without a word, she turned and ran.

Colby tried to go after her, but Mark and Tyler blocked his path, their expressions grim. I didn't stick around to see what happened next. Instead, I dashed after Tara, my heart pounding in my chest.

Soon after, I found her under a tree, her shoulders shaking with sobs. The sight of her crying broke my heart. I wanted to reach out, to comfort her, but I was afraid. Afraid that she would reject me, that she would hate me for revealing the truth in such a brutal manner.

So, I stood there, under the tree, watching as she cried. The sun had set, and the world was bathed in the soft glow of the moon. It was a beautiful scene, marred only by the heartbreak that was unfolding before me.

Seeing her there, crumpled and weeping beneath the tree, was like a punch to the gut. I approached slowly, cautiously, as if she were a wounded animal that might startle and bolt. But when I reached her, she didn't pull away. Instead, she fell into me, her arms wrapping around my waist as she buried her face in my chest.

My heart pounded against my rib cage, the rhythm erratic and wild. I hesitated for a moment, then wrapped my arms around her, holding her close.

"Tara," I murmured, my voice barely above a whisper.

I could feel her tears soaking through the fabric of my pink top, each one a tiny, warm droplet of her pain.

"Don't cry for him," I said, my voice soft but firm.

"He's not worth it. Neither of them are."

She sobbed into my chest, her body shaking with the intensity of her tears. But slowly, as my words sunk in, her sobs began to subside. She lifted her head from my chest, her tear-streaked face tilted up towards mine. Her eyes, usually so bright and vivacious, were dull and red-rimmed from crying.

Something inside me snapped then. Seeing her so hurt, so broken... it was too much. I reached up, my fingers gently brushing away the tear tracks staining her cheeks.

"Tara," I whispered again.

And then I was leaning in, my heart pounding in my ears, my breath hitching in my throat. I could see the surprise in her eyes, but she didn't pull away. Instead, she closed her eyes, her lashes fanning out against her cheeks.

Our lips met in a soft, chaste kiss. It was tentative at first, a gentle exploration, but it quickly deepened. Her arms tightened around me, pulling me closer, and I responded in kind, my arms wrapping around her waist as I lost myself in the taste of her lips.

Eventually, we pulled apart, both of us panting

lightly. She looked up at me, her eyes wide and vulnerable.

"Britney..." she started, but I shook my head.

"Let's just forget about them," I said softly, my thumb gently brushing over her bottom lip.

"You deserve so much better, Tara."

And at that moment, as she nodded and buried her face back in my chest, I knew I would do whatever it took to make her believe that.

Chapter 9

∞∞∞

THREE DAYS HAD passed since that emotionally charged moment beneath the tree. Three days since Tara and I had shared our most passionate kiss. And in those three days, something had shifted between us. I was no longer just Brent, the no-name nerd turned cheerleader, but Britney, Tara's partner, both in the cheerleading squad and off it. We were officially an item.

Our steps were synchronized as we strolled down the school corridor, our skirts swishing in harmony, the fabric whispering secrets to the tiled floor. We wore different tops, mine a royal blue that matched my eyes, and hers a fiery red that complemented her fiery spirit. The halls were alive with the chatter of students, the rhythmic lockers opening and closing, and the occasional laughter echoing off the lockers, but we moved through it all in our own bubble, our hands linked together.

As we approached the cafeteria, Jessica and Colby stepped into our path. Her smug grin was as polished as her scaly snakeskin, and she had her arm looped through Colby's, who looked as if he'd rather be anywhere else.

"What the sissy-lesbian pairing is going on?" she sneered, her eyes raking over us, her lips twisted into an ugly smirk.

The words were meant to wound, to embarrass, but I didn't feel the sting. Not when Tara was by my side, her grip on my hand firm and reassuring.

Without missing a beat, she shot back, "Oh, what the gay jock beard and snake pairing is going on?" Her voice was loud enough to carry across the hallway, and a hush fell over the surrounding students.

A collective gasp echoed around us, followed by a smattering of laughter. Jessica's face turned a shade that matched Tara's skirt, and Colby looked like he'd been sucker-punched. They quickly moved out of our way, disappearing into the throng of students.

Laughing, Tara and I continued towards the cafeteria, our steps light. I turned to her, a grin splitting my face.

"That was so good," I told her, my voice filled with admiration.

She flashed me a triumphant smile, her eyes sparkling with mischief and satisfaction. It was moments like these that made me fall for her even more, moments where she stood up for herself, for us, without a hint of hesitation.

And as we stepped into the cafeteria, the clamor of lunchtime chatter filling our ears, the savory aroma of today's lunch menu wafting through the air, I knew that no matter what came next, I had Tara by my side. And that was more than enough.

We had just settled at our usual table in the cafeteria when Lily and Sarah arrived, their cheerleader skirts swirling about their legs as they sauntered over. I could hear the clatter of trays, the low hum of chatter, and the occasional laughter around us, but it felt like we were in our own world.

Lily was in a white button-up paired with her cheerleading skirt, her hair tied up in a high ponytail, while Sarah wore a fitted green top that complemented her skin beautifully. They slid into the bench opposite us, their eyes lighting up with the same excitement that had been bubbling within me.

"Prom dresses!" Sarah announced dramatically, her eyes sparkling with excitement.

"We need to pick out the hottest dresses. Jessica the snake shouldn't be the prom queen!"

Sarah's words set off a flurry of excitement around the table. Tara's eyes met mine, a spark of anticipation evident in their depths. The air was electric with the prospect of the upcoming prom.

"I've always dreamt of wearing a princess-style dress," Lily confessed, her eyes going dreamy.

"Something in pastel pink, with a tulle skirt and a sweetheart neckline."

"I think I'd look killer in a red dress," Sarah chimed in, already picturing herself in it.

My mind raced with the possibilities, images of dresses in all colors and shapes filling my thoughts. I could see myself in a flowing chiffon number, or maybe something a bit bolder, like a sequin dress. But more than that, I could see Tara, radiant and stunning, making every head turn as she walked in.

The conversation flowed like a river, ideas bouncing around the table as we discussed everything from dress styles to matching accessories. The taste of the cafeteria pizza was forgotten as I got lost in the excitement of it all.

As the lunch period ended, we had a plan in place. We were going to go shopping after school, ready to find the perfect dresses for our prom night. The bell rang, cutting through our excited chatter, and we gathered our trays, our hearts full of anticipation.

Walking out of the cafeteria, I felt a rush of excitement course through me. For the first time in my life, I was looking forward to shopping for a dress, a girl's dress. And the best part was, I'd be doing it with Tara, Sarah, and Lily. We were going to make this prom a night to remember.

The moment we piled into Tara's pink convertible, Sarah connected her phone to the car's Bluetooth and started playing Kim Petras' 'Heart to Break'. The song quickly filled the car, creating an atmosphere of excited anticipation.

Tara's fingers drummed on the steering

wheel, keeping rhythm with the beat, while Lily and Sarah started singing along, their voices harmonizing perfectly with the catchy tune. I found myself joining in, my voice blending with theirs as we belted out the lyrics together.

The wind whipped through my blonde wig as we sped down the road, the scent of Tara's vanilla perfume mixing with the fresh air. I could taste the lingering sweetness of the cherry lip gloss I had applied earlier and feel the rush of adrenaline as we approached the mall.

As the final chorus of 'Heart to Break' filled the car, Tara pulled into a parking spot and killed the engine. The sudden silence felt heavy after the loud music, but it was quickly filled with our laughter as we tumbled out of the car. The scent of the mall hit me then, a mixture of perfume, food, and new clothes that always made me feel excited.

We ventured into the vast expanse of the mall, our eyes sparkling with the thrill of the hunt. There were so many stores to choose from, and we had all afternoon.

Our first stop was a boutique known for its stunning prom dresses. Tara led the way, her confidence radiating around her. I followed behind her, trying to match her stride. Sarah and Lily were chattering excitedly behind me, their voices a comforting presence.

Inside the boutique, racks upon racks of dresses greeted us, a sea of colors and fabrics that made my head spin. The scent of new fabric and the faint hint of perfume filled the air. I watched as Tara immediately started pulling dresses off the racks, her expert eyes scanning the selection.

I picked up a soft chiffon dress, the fabric cool and smooth under my fingers. It was a beautiful blush pink, with delicate lace detailing on the bodice and a flowing skirt. I held it up against myself, glancing at my reflection in a nearby mirror.

Sarah spotted me and rushed over, her eyes lighting up at the sight of the dress.

"That looks amazing on you, Britney!" She exclaimed, her enthusiasm infectious. I felt a warm flush of pride, my heart pounding with excitement.

We spent hours in the boutique, trying on dress after dress. The sound of laughter echoed off the walls as we twirled in front of mirrors and helped each other zip up gowns. Each dress brought a new wave of excitement, a new potential for the perfect prom look.

As the day wore on, we finally settled on our dresses. Tara chose a stunning green dress that hugged her curves and made her eyes sparkle. Lily found her dream princess-style dress in a beautiful shade of pastel pink. Sarah looked killer indeed in a bold, red bodycon dress that made her look like a Hollywood starlet. And me? I ended up with the blush pink chiffon dress, its softness and elegance making me feel like a princess.

With our dresses safely bagged and in our hands, we left the boutique, feeling victorious and exhilarated. The mall was closing, and the lights were dimming, casting a warm glow over everything. We made our way back to the car, our hearts light and our spirits high.

As we pulled away from the mall, Kim Petras' 'Heart to Break' started playing once more. This time, however, it felt like a victory anthem. We sang along, our voices echoing in the night as we drove towards our respective homes. I couldn't help but feel a sense of contentment, a feeling of belonging.

The next day, the rhythm of Mr. Miller's lecture on quantum mechanics was playing a lullaby to my ears, lulling me into a trance. My fingers fiddled with the edge of my textbook, the sharp corners biting into my skin. I was struggling to focus, the room around me was nothing but a blur.

Suddenly, the blaring sound of the school

intercom coming to life jolted me out of my stupor. The whole room went silent, each student holding their breath as Principal Hawkins' voice filled the room.

"Good morning, students. It's time to announce the nominees for this year's Prom King and Queen." There was a pause, and I could hear my heartbeat pounding in my ears. I felt Tara squeeze my hand under the desk, her fingers warm and comforting against mine.

"For Prom King, the nominees are Colby Fletcher, Tyler Swan, Harold Lang, Dirk Lee, and... Sam Stockton." The room erupted into cheers and whistles, the boys slapping each other's backs and grinning.

The room buzzed with excitement as Principal Hawkins moved on to the nominees for Prom Queen.

"And for Prom Queen, we have Tara Adams," cheers erupted around the room, and I squeezed Tara's hand back, a proud smile on my face, "Sarah Sinclair, Lily Sparks, Jessica Woods, and..." there was a moment of silence, the room holding its breath, "Britney Lowes."

The room exploded, cheers and claps echoing off the walls. I was frozen in my seat, my heart pounding in my chest. I could hear my name being chanted by my classmates, a sea of faces turned towards me. I was in shock, my mind racing. I was a nominee for Prom Queen.

I looked over at Tara, her face was glowing with excitement, her eyes sparkling with pride. She threw her arms around me, hugging me tightly. I could smell her sweet vanilla perfume, the scent enveloping me.

I was brought back to reality by the sound of my classmates cheering. They were on their feet, applauding and whistling, their voices filling the room. I could feel my face burning, the heat spreading through my body.

The rest of the day was a blur, a whirlwind of congratulations and excited chatter. I felt like I was in a dream, floating on a cloud of disbelief and excitement. Every time someone mentioned the prom, my heart would flutter, the anticipation building inside me.

As I walked home that day, the sun setting and casting a warm glow over the town, I replayed the day's events in my mind. I was a nominee for Prom Queen. I was going to the prom with Tara. I was living a life I never thought I'd have the chance to live. And for the first time in a long time, I felt truly happy.

That night, as I lay in bed, my mind was filled with thoughts of the prom. I could see myself in my pink chiffon dress, Tara by my side. I could feel the excitement in the air, the anticipation building as the announcement for Prom Queen was made. And even though I didn't know what the future held, I knew one thing for sure. I was going to enjoy every moment of it.

Chapter 10

∞∞∞

I T WAS A TYPICAL SUNDAY NIGHT, the aroma of Mom's homemade lasagna wafting through the house, colliding with the steady hum of Dad's football game blaring from the TV. We were all gathered around the dining table, Christina, Mom, Dad, and me. I had a heavy lump in my throat, my stomach churning with nerves. I had something to tell them, something that had been weighing on my mind for the past week.

"Dad, Mom, Chris," I started, my voice shaking slightly, "I have something to tell you." They all turned to look at me, their eyes filled with curiosity. I took a deep breath, steeling myself for their reactions, "I'm going to prom."

Mom clapped her hands together, a wide smile on her face, "That's wonderful, Brent!" Dad nodded, his eyes crinkling at the corners with pride.

"But," I continued, my heart pounding in my chest, "I'm not going as Brent. I'm going as Britney."

There was a silence, and for a moment, I thought I'd made a terrible mistake. But then, my sister broke into a grin, "I knew it!" she exclaimed, "Sarah already told me, but I wanted you to tell us yourself."

"There's nothing to be afraid of," Dad said, his voice choked with emotion. His eyes were shining, and I could tell he meant every word. Mom reached across the table to squeeze my hand, her touch warm and comforting.

"The truth is, I've been dressing up as a girl, and going to cheer practice as Britney." I admitted, my heart pounding in my chest.

Mom nodded, her eyes filled with understanding.

"And that's why you've been growing your hair out?"

I nodded, feeling a weight lifting off my shoulders. Their acceptance meant more to me than anything else in the world.

The following day, Christina and I embarked on a prom preparation marathon. We hit her closet, sifting through an ocean of lace and satin. She picked a matching blush-colored bra and panty set, her enthusiasm infectious.

"This will look fabulous on you, Britney," she said, her eyes sparkling.

Next was the makeup tutorial. She was my guide, her hands deft as she showed me how to apply foundation, create a soft smoky eye look, and paint my lips a rosy pink.

"Always remember to blend, blend, blend," she instructed, her tone patient yet firm.

"I already know that, sis," I bragged.

We moved onto the wig, a high-quality blonde piece that my girlfriend gave me. She helped me secure it, her nimble fingers adjusting it until it sat perfectly on my head.

"You look stunning, Britney," she affirmed, her words boosting my confidence.

The grand finale was the dress. A soft pink chiffon piece that flowed around me like a gentle breeze. She helped me into a shapewear, its tight embrace sculpting a more feminine silhouette.

"This is it, Britney," she exclaimed, her excitement palpable.

As I looked at my reflection, I saw Britney, beautiful and ready for prom. Ready to be seen, to be accepted, and to love herself openly. With my family's unwavering support, I knew I could face whatever the prom night had in store for me.

Moments later, it was a symphony of nervous anticipation, the faint beat of my heart against the silence of the night. I stood on the porch, my family beside me, awaiting Tara's arrival. The purr of a car engine echoed in the distance, and soon a pink convertible rolled into the driveway. She stepped out, a vision in a sparkly green dress, her smile as radiant as the stars above.

"Hi, Mrs. Lowes, Mr. Lowes, Christina," she greeted my family. She then turned to me, her eyes sparkling with a softness that made my heart flutter.

"Hi, babe," she said, her voice soft as satin.

"Hey babe," I returned, my voice barely above a whisper. We shared a look, a silent exchange of understanding, then interlaced our fingers. With my family's warm goodbyes ringing in our ears, we descended into the inviting comfort of her car.

The ride to the prom was a blur of soft whispers and stolen glances. The scent of her perfume wafted around me, a sweet blend of vanilla and roses. We talked about everything and nothing, our nerves slowly dissolving into the night. The lights of the school danced in the distance, and before we knew it, we were there.

"You ready for this, Brit?"

"As ready as I'll ever be!" I said before contaminating my lipgloss with her red lipstick.

Hand-in-hand, we entered the school gym, transformed into a fairytale castle for the night. The crowd buzzed with excitement, the air filled with the heady scent of anticipation. Our classmates turned to greet us, their smiles warm and welcoming.

Sarah and Lily arrived next, both in a stunning array of sequins and chiffon. Sarah was with Tyler Swan, and Lily was on the arm of Harold Lang.

"Oh... my... God! Don't we all look I-C-O-N-I-C?" Sarah chanted.

"Yes, and woah, Britney!" Tyler said.

"Ugh! Shut up, Ty!" Lily followed with a jealous tone.

The four of us exchanged excited smiles and compliments, the bond of friendship warming the air around us.

"You're perfect," I whispered to Tara as we made our way to the table, the girls' dresses billowing around them, their dates trailing behind. The table was a bedazzlement of glittering tablecloth and candlelight, the soft glow of the candles reflecting off the sequins of our dresses.

Just as we settled down, Jessica and Colby walked in, their presence like a cloud casting a shadow over our excitement. Jessica wore a black dress that clung to her like a second skin, her hair cascading over her shoulders. Colby was in a black suit, his expression a mixture of arrogance and unease. Their eyes fell on us, their lips curling into a smirk, their laughter echoing in the air.

"Look at the LGBTQIA+ community hoping for a shot at prom queen," Jessica said.

"Yeah, and you're the biggest ally with your gay boyfriend pretending to be straight for the title," Tyler shot back. Colby almost jumped out of his position but Jessica stopped her.

"What a hypocrite," Tara said.

We didn't let them dampen our spirits. We clung onto each other, our camaraderie our strength against their disdain. We were here to celebrate us, not them. And no amount of snide remarks or smug looks could change that.

The anticipation in the room was almost tangible, a thick fog of excitement that hung heavily over us. We were huddled at our table, hands clasped together, as the principal took to the stage. His voice echoed around the room, the words 'prom king and queen' ringing in my ears.

"And the prom king is... Colby Fletcher!" The crowd erupted into applause, and I watched as he took the stage, a smug smile playing on his lips. I glanced at Tara, her expression unreadable.

"Now for the prom queen... the anticipation is killing me," the principal joked, pulling out the envelope. A hush fell over the crowd, everyone leaning forward in their seats. I could feel my heart pounding in my chest, the world around me fading into a dull hum.

"And the prom queen is... Britney Lowes!" The crowd erupted into applause once again, but this time, it was a mixture of shock and delight. I looked around, unable to believe my ears.

Jessica stood up, her face a mask of disbelief.

"That's not fair! She's not even a girl!" she shrieked, pointing at me. A chorus of boos filled the air, and the principal signaled for security. She was escorted out, her tantrum echoing through the room.

"This is not right! Abomination!" she screamed.

I made my way to the stage, my legs shaking beneath me. I took the microphone, my voice echoing around the room.

"Thank you, everyone. But I believe there's someone more deserving of this crown." I turned to Tara, her eyes wide with surprise.

"Tara, would you join me here?"

Tears welled up in her eyes as she ascended the stage, the crowd cheering her on. I placed the crown on her head, the sparkling tiara fitting perfectly atop her scarlet curls. The applause was deafening, and I couldn't help but beam at her, her joy contagious.

Colby stepped forward then, his gaze falling on me and Tara.

"I'm sorry, Tara. I'm sorry, Brent, I mean, Britney" he said, his voice surprisingly sincere.

"I think you deserve this more than me."

With that, he placed the king's crown on

my head, the weight of it a sweet victory. The crowd erupted into applause again, our classmates chanting our names.

The principal then announced, "Let's get the party started!" and the room was flooded with music. Tara and I took to the dance floor, our bodies swaying in time with the rhythm. Our eyes locked, and I could see the stars reflected in her gaze.

"You look beautiful tonight, Tara," I whispered, my heart pounding in my chest.

"You look beautiful too, Britney," she replied, a soft smile playing on her lips.

Our faces drew closer, our breaths mingling in the space between us. And then, we kissed, the world fading away as we lost ourselves in each other. The crowd cheered around us, but all I could see was Tara. And at that moment, I knew I wouldn't have it any other way.

Chapter 11

∞∞∞

OUR LIPS LINGERED IN A KISS that felt like it spanned a lifetime. My senses were filled with Tara—the sweet taste of her cherry lips, the softness of her skin, the floral scent of her perfume. Each touch was an electric current that set my veins alight, my heart thumping in my chest like a wild drum.

We broke apart slowly, our foreheads resting together as we caught our breath. Her eyes sparkled with a mischievous glint as she took my hand, leading us towards her pink convertible parked nearby. The night was warm, the soft wind carrying the intoxicating scent of blooming flowers as it played with the hem of our dresses.

"Britney," she murmured, her voice barely

above a whisper as she opened the car door for me. I slid into the passenger seat, my heart pounding in my chest. She got in after me, her gaze never leaving mine as she started the car.

The drive was a blur of city lights and soft music playing from the radio. My senses were heightened, every beat of the song pulsating through my veins, every brush of her fingers against mine sending shivers down my spine.

We parked in a desolate area, the moonlight casting a soft glow over the surrounding trees. She turned off the car, the silence enveloping us. Her eyes were a pool of emotions, her lips slightly parted as if she was about to say something.

The tension was palpable, a magnetic pull that I couldn't resist. I leaned over the console, my hand reaching out to gently brush a loose curl from her face. She closed her eyes, leaning into my touch, her breath hitching in her throat.

"Britney," she whispered, her voice shaking. "I... I..."

I cut her off with a kiss, unable to bear the anticipation any longer. The kiss was passionate, our bodies leaning into each other as if we were two halves of a whole. I could feel her heartbeat against mine, the rhythm matching the frantic pace of my own.

We broke apart, our breaths coming out in pants. Her eyes were filled with desire, her lips slightly swollen from our kiss. I felt a surge of affection for her, my heart swelling in my chest.

"I love you, Tara," I confessed, the words falling from my lips before I could stop them.

Her eyes widened in surprise, her lips parting in a silent gasp. A beat passed, and then another. I was about to apologize, to take back my words when she threw her arms around me, her lips crashing onto mine.

"I love you too, Britney, make love to me," she murmured against my lips, her confession sending waves of warmth through my body.

I was still in disbelief, here I was, about to have sex with the most popular girl in school in her pink convertible in our prom dresses. My tucked penis was fighting my panties from how beautifully her red locks moved against her opulent cleavage.

I leaned in, my hormones overcoming my inhibitions, and kissed her—relishing her warm tongue glide over my lips. I then parted them and got lost in her taste. We were so fixated on making out that we barely noticed that anyone could catch us.

"I'm a virgin," she shyly said. How could the most popular girl in school be a virgin? I briefly thought. But then, I realized, I was a virgin too and

I had no idea what I was going to do. I had to make her first time memorable.

She started caressing my cock underneath my dress against my panties and it was the most tactile sensation I'd felt in my life. My penis was going crazy and I was about two seconds away from ejaculating.

"You better not cum inside," she said, "I'm not on the pill."

"Right," I said, calming down a bit. Her fingers traveled to the waistband of my panties and she started pulling. Soon after, my cock sprang out, almost out of my dress entirely.

"Whoa, it's bigger than I thought," she said.

"Wait, do you want to do this?" I was still hoping she'd change her mind but also hoping she didn't.

"Of course, I've been dreaming of this day my whole life," she said.

I slipped my hand under her dress, between her tits, I could feel her nipples harden as my fingers came in contact with her skin. Soon after, I put my hand on her stomach, feeling her smooth curves and her panties. I could feel her heartbeat and her warm and soft skin. I found the crevice between her legs and felt her pussy mound and a small patch of hair.

Rubbing her clit—she pressed her pussy against my hand. The feeling of it against my hand was amazing and I could do nothing but bask in her warmth. I'd never touched a woman before and I just realized how much I'd been missing.

She leaned over and completely removed my panties. I couldn't believe it, I was finally going to have sex.

"I'm going to make you feel so good," I whispered in her ear—not sure as to where I got the unfound confidence from.

She started kissing me on my neck, the feeling of her lips on my body felt magical, I imagined that this is what angels must feel. I couldn't believe what was happening to me.

"Let's go to the backseat," she said. We both scooted over to the backseat of her car so we could lie down. I wanted to see her beautiful breasts first —sure enough, they looked even more beautiful with the outside light hitting them and her nipples were on point.

I took a moment to look around, and we were alone. We were far enough away from town that no one was going to see us. I pulled her thong to the side and felt her clit with my fingers then she started softly moaning.

Soon after, I began sucking on her nipple and she let out a moan.

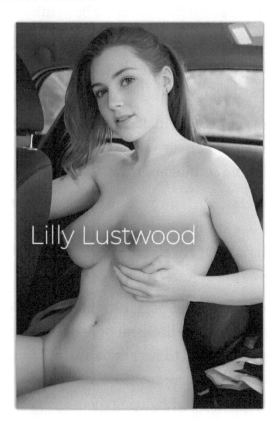

"Mmm! Yes, yes, yes!" she cheered.

My cock grew harder and started to throb. As I sucked on her nipple, I could feel her hand begin to move down my body then she squeezed my ass and kissed my neck.

I could already feel pre-cum leaking out of my cock as she squeezed it.

"Mmm... this feels like a dream," she said.

I moved my finger down and felt her wetness then I moved my finger inside her—causing her to gasp like a fish out of water. I wanted to feel her tight pussy wrapped around my cock so bad but I didn't want to rush the experience.

Leaning in, I started lightly kissing her breasts. Her nipples pointed straight at me—that particular imagery was so erotic. Her warm, soft skin and my magical lips against her body was the best feeling in the world.

I continued to tease her pussy with my finger as I kissed her as she moaned softly. Suddenly, she grabbed the bottom of her dress and pulled it up, exposing her perfect pink pussy. I couldn't believe how beautiful she looked.

"Oh my god, Tara, you are so tight," I said as I slipped my finger inside her pussy. It felt so amazing and warm. I couldn't believe this was really happening.

"I'm a virgin," she reminded.

"I know, I'm your first," I said.

"I want you to be my first everything," she said, kissing me.

As I kissed down to her stomach, I could see her pussy glisten with arousal. I could also see how strong her clit was—telling me that she was ready to be taken. She spread her legs and I could feel her pussy with my fingers—I wanted to eat her pussy so bad I could almost taste it.

As I kissed the inside of her thighs, my cock throbbed harder and harder. My fingers started caressing her clit with perfect timing with my tongue. I started eating her pussy and licking her juices.

"Fuck, yeah!"

She started cooing and moaning louder as I fingered her. I couldn't believe how wet she was. I'd never seen a vagina this wet before even in porn that I was beginning to doubt I was even doing it right.

But I was loving it and she was enjoying it.

I began lightly grinding my cock against her thigh trying to gain the most pleasure. She pushed me back against the seat and began kissing my chest and neck.

"I've wanted this for so long," she whispered.

She started kissing my nipples the sucked on them. They were so sensated and I didn't want her to stop. I wanted her to do it forever. The feeling was so intense that I wanted to cum.

She began rubbing my cock against her pussy and I was so close to cumming that I didn't know what to do.

"I want you to make love to me," she said.

"I will," I said, kissing her.

"I've never done it before so you'll have to take it slow."

"I promise." I replied.

I put her legs over my shoulders and positioned my cock at her pussy entrance. She was so wet that my cockhead was covered in her pussy juices, it looked like she'd already been fucked.

Inserting my cock in her pussy—I felt like I was swimming in the pacific ocean during a summer break. It was warm, wet, and tight. It was like heaven. I was slowly pushing my cock into her and it was the most amazing feeling of my life.

"Ahh!" I let out a guttural groan.

The tip of my cock was in her and I could feel her pussy walls gripping me. I wanted to push further. As I did, we became locked into a kiss and her legs wrapped around my back, pushing me against her.

I started pushing further into her and I was almost half-way in her.

"Mmm, yes, it feels so good!" she yelled--her face almost as red as her hair.

As I slowly began thrusting, it got better and better. The warmth and tightness of her pussy was perfect.

"Yes, that feels so nice... ugh," she continued.

"Keep fucking me, just like that," she murmured.

As I thrust into her pussy, I could feel her juices covering my cock. It felt so amazing. Her pussy was just perfect, I felt like I was lost in an orgasmic dream.

"Oh my god!" she moaned.

"You like this?" I asked, increasing the pressure.

"Mmm, yes, keep doing it."

Her eyes were closed and I could tell she was totally into it. I was worried I wouldn't last long but I wanted to make her feel good. She opened her eyes and looked at me.

"Yes, it feels so perfect, ahhh..." she breathed—her eyes glistening.

I could feel her pussy start to spasm and I knew she was cumming because she cooed like a dove.

"Ohhhh... I'm cumming—baby, I'm cumming!" she said loudly.

Her pussy vibrated and squeezed my cock so tightly that I moaned in pleasure. I couldn't hold it in any longer.

We were both moaning and gasping for breath

as I was sliding in and out of her. I couldn't believe what I was doing and neither could she. She was a fucking virgin and I was giving her her first sexual experience and I couldn't believe how much of a turn on it was.

Without me realizing it, our thrusts began to sync up perfectly. It was like we had been lovers our whole lives.

"I'm gonna cum! I'm gonna!" but before I could finish my orgasmic recitation, she pulled away and pointed my dick at her tits. As I shivered in euphoria, I watched my cock paint her flawless breasts with my thick white cream.

"Mmm, Britney, pretty little Britney..." she said as I collapsed on top of her.

"That was... insane!" I said with a gasp.

As we kissed under the starlit sky, I knew that I had found my home in Tara. The girl who saw me for who I truly was, who loved me despite my flaws, who stood by my side through thick and thin. And I couldn't have asked for anything more.

Epilogue

∞∞∞

THE FINAL CHAPTER of my high school journey was upon me. There I was, Britney Lowes, standing at the edge of the mat, trembling with a mix of fear and excitement. The roar of the crowd was deafening, their thunderous applause and chants echoing off the walls of the stadium. The music, so loud it rattled my bones, thrummed with a rhythm that matched the pounding of my heart.

"Gold Lions, Gold Lions," the crowd chanted, their voices blending into a symphony of anticipation. I took a deep breath, steadying my nerves. The smell of sweat, rubber mats, and hairspray filled my nostrils.

My cheer uniform, a blend of green and gold,

felt like a second skin. My hair, dyed blonde and styled perfectly, made me feel secure. My makeup, expertly applied by Tara, shimmered under the harsh stadium lights.

Beside me, Tara gripped my hand, her own nerves mirrored in her eyes. She gave my hand a reassuring squeeze, her smile wide and bright.

"Concord Briggs High School," the announcer's voice boomed over the speakers, the crowd roaring their approval. The words sent a shiver down my spine, the reality of the situation sinking in. We were about to perform in the National Cheering Championship.

The music started, a high-energy beat that vibrated through the air. My heart pounded in time with the rhythm, adrenaline coursing through my veins. I glanced one last time at Tara before we moved into position.

The routine was a blur of flips, jumps, and stunts. The crowd's cheers fueled us, their energy radiating off them in waves. My body moved on instinct, months of practice guiding me through the complex routine.

Then, before I knew it, I had to fly.

At the top of the pyramid, I took a deep breath.

"3-2-1..." my voice barely above a whisper. Tyler and Mark threw me like a basketball—causing me to soar high like an eagle. Shortly after, our routine was over.

The crowd was on their feet, their cheers deafening. I was panting, my body slick with sweat, but a wide smile was plastered on my face. Tara was beside me, her arms wrapped around me in a tight hug.

The anticipation was thick in the air as we waited for the results. The announcer's voice echoed around the stadium, the crowd falling silent.

"And the winner of the National Cheering Championship is..." there was a pause, the suspense nearly unbearable, "Concord Briggs High School!"

The crowd erupted in cheers, their applause deafening. Tara and I screamed in joy, our bodies shaking with excitement. We had done it. We had won.

As I stood there, clutching her in my arms, a wave of pride washed over me. I was Britney, a cheerleader, a prom queen, and a champion. I had faced my fears, embraced my true self, and had come out victorious.

THE END <3

Did you enjoy Cheerleader By Chance? In that case, I hope you could check out my bundle Girlification 1.

It contains five of my chart-topping illustrated feminization and transgender transformation steamy romances.

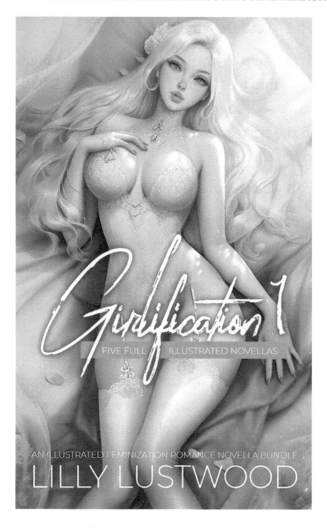

Story 1 – Sissified in Mars

From a small male Earthling to the Queen of Mars, I, Elona Max, will tell you a story of Love, Sacrifice, and the Power of the Feminine Spirit.

Story 2 – Let's Get Physical

With the help of my workmates from the Big Boys gym, I didn't only unleash the talent I had for creating choreography, but I also discovered that I had the perfect body for tight pink leggings and sports bra.

Story 3 – Dangerous Disguise

The death toll was rising and I had to do something. With a series of ignored killings, I decided to go undercover and find the criminal in my blonde wig and high-heeled boots.

Story 4 – New Wardrobe

As I slipped into the character of Bonnie, I found myself captivated by the art of transformation. With each layer of makeup, every stroke of the brush, and the careful selection of wigs, lingerie, and clothing, I felt my true self emerging. The sensation of satin against my skin and the gentle sway of my hips in a skirt awakened a desire that I couldn't ignore.

Story 5 – Cyber Babe

As I became more and more obsessed with her, I found myself dressing up and transforming into her, embracing every curve and stitch of her digital persona.

Clutch your Pearl Necklace Tight and Prepare for a Feminization Romance Ride!

Note: This collection contains feminization, transgender transformation, romance, and first time with a transgender woman tropes.

Read Girlification 1

Book Bundles

∞ ∞ ∞

Need more of my romantic bedtime stories? It's your lucky day! All of my bundles are unique, and none of the stories were cross-added so you can buy all of them without having to worry about whether or not a story already appeared on another bundle.

With these bundles, you're going to save more than 50%. Love love love!

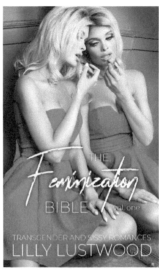

Custom Story

∞ ∞ ∞

Did you know that I also write custom/ commission-based stories? Yes, I do, and I will write it to the tee based on your liking. Here's a sample of a commission story I've created for one of my lovely readers.

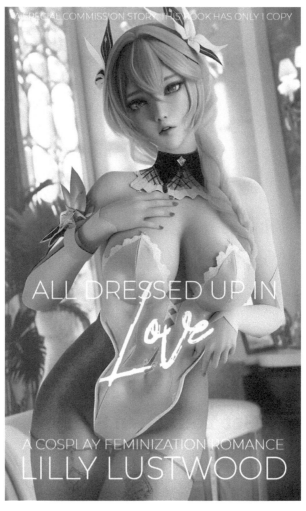

Added to that, if you're a Lilly Lustwood reader, you're quite aware of how colorful my prose is and I do three rounds of edits before I publish. Please understand that masterpieces cannot be rushed.

Don't take my word for it, here's what one of them had to say:

"I love the story!!!! Ty for writing almost 100 pages for Michelle and Evelynn—I'm sure they're happy you gave them such love and attention as well. <3 My only disappointment came when I finished reading, but I realized I can re-read as much as I want.

Your storytelling skills are so great—if there's any way I can leave a review please let me know! I truly enjoyed every moment of this commission." -Michelle

Get Your Own Story

Audiobooks

∞ ∞ ∞

I know that many of you prefer consuming a book while doing something else. Most especially when it's some of my books which are hard to read even with one hand haha!

That's why I've created audiobook versions of my top sellers. They're available on Audible and other major distributors!

Listen to Audiobooks

Sissy Store

Lilly's Choice
SISSY TOYS & CLOTHES
FOR FEMININE BOYS

Many of my readers love dressing up. What inspired me to create the Sissy Store is the e-mails I've received from them wanting to emulate the characters in my story.

And the best way to do that? Dressing up of course! That's why I made the Sissy Store, it's a curation of my favorite finds online to provide you with an easier time in shopping for the best outfits available.

From wigs, breastplates, stockings, and down to shoes, toys, uniforms, lingerie, and more, you'll find everything you need!

Visit The Sissy Store

Other Titles

THE COMPLETE AND DEFINITIVE GUIDE TO TOTAL FEMINIZATION

LILLY LUSTWOOD 2 NIKKI CRESCENT

THE GIRLY GUIDE

INCLUDES TIPS, AFFIRMATIONS, & 250+ PHOTOS

"The only Feminization Guide you'll ever need."

Read The Girly Guide 2

"You can't be serious. How can I become an Avon Lady when I'm CLEARLY a guy?"

Read All Made Up

"Underneath her pencil skirt and silk blouse, distracting all the yearning men in the conference room with her apparition, she knew exactly who to give her attention to for her next career opportunity."

Read The Office Gurl

"There's that voice again... telling me to swipe the scarlet rouge on my lips, wear my mother's dress, and go to the nearest bar in my red stilettos".

Read Femininely Possessed

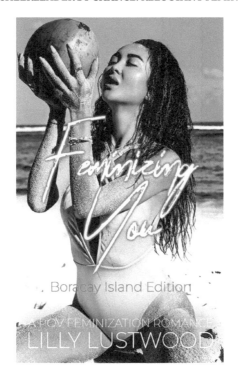

"It's your feminization story, I just wrote it for you, xoxo Lilly."

Read Feminizing You

"I have two pieces of good news, first, you're not going to school anymore, and second, you're hired as a new maid!"

"My father wouldn't allow this!"

"Enough with the drama, slide on those Mary Janes!"

Read Sissyrella

Author's Message

Dear Romantic Reader,

Thank you very much for purchasing and reading *Cheerleader By Chance- Reluctant Feminization and*

Transgender Romance.

For a writer, I can't seem to find the best word to describe how grateful I am for your support.

If you enjoyed this book, KINDLY **(with puppy-dog eyes) give it a Rating and Review it on Kindle.**

Let's get it to the overall bestseller list <3

Should you feel the need to send me a message concerning this book, your love life, or just about anything, please feel free to follow the pages below and Subscribe to my Mailing List to get updates on Free Books, Promos, and New Releases.

You can also follow my author profile on Amazon simply by visiting the Amazon Page below, you will get e-mails from Amazon whenever I have a new book, xo.

Mailing List (stats.sender.net/forms/er756a/view)

Home Page (www.lillylustwood.wordpress.com)

Amazon Page (www.amazon.com/Lilly-Lustwood/e/B0B9X11BMR/)

Facebook | Twitter | TikTok (@LillyLustwood)

Goodreads (www.goodreads.com/lillylustwood)

Made in United States
Troutdale, OR
02/03/2024

17409726R00119